# W.O.O.F.

Women of Overcoming Faith

\*\*\*\*\*\*\*\*\*\*\*\*

A Novel by
Bestselling Author

## Jeanetta Britt

Published by Twelve Stones Publishing LLC
Eufaula, Alabama
www.jbrittbooks.com
brittbooks@msn.com
Library of Congress Control Number: 2020901952
ISBN 978-1-7327071-4-6
Revised Edition 2020

Editors: Glorias Dixon, Fairrene Carter-Frost
Cover: Michelle Stimpson

# LOVE NOTES

I had the extreme pleasure of attending the Community Healing Network, Inc. workshop held on the campus of Tuskegee University in 2009. (Learn more at: www.communityhealingnet.org)

At that time, I had contemplated this story for over five years, but was reticent to write it because I knew for it to be compelling--more than just another *church* book--there had to be strong characters--women--with real issues from which they needed to be healed. It was at the afternoon session of the workshop that I was finally convinced that this story is worth telling.

You see, a bus-load of young people and their chaperones from the GodParents Youth Organization joined us unexpectedly for lunch and the afternoon session. (Learn more about GodParents at: www.godparentsclub.org) And as a means of inspiring the youth, and indeed us all, Sister Trina Cashaw Nicholson shared the most intimate details of her childhood and the healing process that had occurred through her walk with the Lord. Now, the wife of a medical doctor with a loving family, her inspiring testimony reminded us that *all* things are possible with God, and it helped convince me that this story of women using the Bible to nurture, support, and heal 'one another' is meaningful.

Thank you, Sister Trina, for your transparency and grace. Your story of healing helps heal us all!

# LOVE LETTERS FROM HOME

© Jeanetta Britt

I read a letter from home today
It was warm, and rich, and sweet
It told me that I was loved
From my head down to my feet.

I read the words with anticipation
They sent chills up and down my spine
And then my soul got happy
And danced with joy divine.

The letter gave me a promise
A blessed assurance while I'm away
It says I can call back home
Each night and every day.

Knowing that I'm cared for
Even while I'm down here
Let's me know I'm not alone
And there's nothing for me to fear.

With the love of my family
In-dwelling my heart
I can feel our close connection
And it keeps us from being apart.

The letters from home I treasure
Like pressed flowers in a book
And they invite me back daily
To simply take a look.

The book, you see, is the Bible
And each chapter and every verse
Is bursting over with love and life
Sent from heaven down here to earth.

Written by my Father
Signed in blood by my Brother
Who delivers them by His Spirit
To my heart, like none other.

But no need to worry
You can read them, too
God's love letters
Are also addressed…to you

*That every one of you should know how to possess his vessel*
*in sanctification and honour...*
*1 Thessalonians 4:4*

# DEDICATION

- To Jason Stewart, Britt Stewart, Carlesa Dixon, Annie Smith, and Johnny Jackson, thanks for your humor. Your unique look at the world makes all our lives a little brighter!

- To Deborah Pearson *(WOOF Radio-99.7 FM, Dothan, AL)*, thank you for your kind encouragement and sisterly support. You are truly a blessing!

- To my Fisk University, Class of 1971, I love each of you with an eternal love. Congratulations on Forty, Fine Years! ***Fisk Forever!!***

# CHAPTER 1: LOVE
## ONE ANOTHER.

*John 13:34*

"Woman!" Her live-in boyfriend snatched her by the collar into a nearby alley out of the earshot of passersby. *Wham!* He smacked her face into the brick wall covered in gang graffiti. "What you doing coming outta that battered women's shelter, huh?" He set her up for the next blow. "I've been looking all over town for you!"

She shrank back from the pain, shielding their four-month-old baby in her arms. "But Quan—"

"But-Quan, nothing!" He barked. "Ain't that big-bank, high-dollar crib I be slangin' drugs night and day to buy you up in Plano, good enough for you?" He raised his hand to smack her again. "Ain't it?"

A single tear trickled from her right eye. If he hadn't been so crazy-mad, he might've noticed that the left eye on her hazelnut face was still swollen nearly shut from their previous encounter—the savage beat-down that had caused her to find refuge at the Heart and Hands Women's Shelter in the first place.

"Ahh, Baby." Quan huffed, thumbing the tear from her face. "It don't have to be like this. Why you always go and make me so mad, huh? Why?"

"But Quan, I don't mean to make you mad." Lily whimpered. "I never mean to make you mad, but you hurt me so very bad. And you promised me…after that last time…you'd never hit me again."

"I know, Lily." Quan pinned his full weight against her on the wall. He was over six feet to her five feet. "And I meant it, Baby. I just had a little too much, you know, hangin' with my homies, not thinking straight." He gyrated his hips against her in an attempt to be sexy.

"Quan—"

"You know you my baby…and Iris, too." He caressed the baby's face, and she looked up at him like he was a stranger. Quan straightened himself and snarled down at Lily again. "That is if Iris really is my baby!"

"Of course, she's yours Quan. Whose else would she be? You know there's nobody for me but you."

"I don't know nothing!" Quan pinned Lily's shoulders against the wall, flexing his tattooed biceps. He was convinced his muscle-bound body art and the neat little twists on his smooth brown head drove the women wild. "How would I know what you *chicken-heads* be doing when I ain't around?" Quan grabbed her up from the wall and shook her like a rag doll. Lily clung to Iris for dear life. "Come on!" He growled. "We're going home."

"But Quan," Lily whispered, "promise me you'll never hit me again."

"Promise you?" Quan pushed her along the cracked sidewalk to his pimped-out Lexus SUV. "You're mine, Woman." He howled. "Like this here ride." Quan pushed her and baby Iris into the passenger seat. "I don't have to promise you nothing!"

Quan threw Lily's bag into the back seat, slid in on the driver's side and slammed the locks shut. He squeezed Lily's chin into one big palm and pulled her nose up to his. "If you ever try a stunt like this again, Woman, I'll kill you and that baby. Do you hear me?"

"Yes, Quan," Lily stuttered, "I hear you."

Quan flipped Lily's face to within an inch of the side window. He licked the tip of his index finger and branded the middle of Iris' forehead with it. "Al-righty-then!" Quan gave his drug-encrusted nostrils a stiff swipe and a hard sniff. "I see you get my point." He cranked up his SUV and squealed out of the parking space, blasting a trail of gangster rap out of his rear speakers.

"Was it your mamma?" Quan started up again as soon as they were underway. "That nosy Mother Brown what gave you the idea you could leave me?" Quan pressed. "Well, was it? Answer me!"

"No, Quan, my mom had nothing to do with it." Lily hugged the passenger door and rocked Iris.

"Then what was it? Talk to me!"

"It's just—"

"Just what? Answer me! Don't make me stop this car!"

"Quan, Baby, I was in pain. I was scared. You've ruined it for me and my mom. I had nowhere else to go."

"I ruined it with your mom. Ha! You was the one that came crawling to my doorstep; remember? Telling me you

3

need me. Telling me you want me. Telling me I was the only one for you. Telling me you love me. Remember? Remember?"

"Yeah, Quan, I did love you." Lily quickly hit rewind. "I do love you, but Baby, I needed stitches after the last time you knocked me around."

"I don't want to hear it! I already apologized for that. Didn't you hear me? Didn't you?"

"Yes." Lily clutched Iris close and rocked her. She didn't want her to start crying, not now.

"Yes, what?"

"Yes, Quan, I heard you apologize."

"And—"

"And I accepted your apology, Baby."

Iris whimpered.

Lily rocked harder.

"What's wrong with her?"

"Nothing, Baby. She probably just wants her bottle. It's in my bag in the backseat."

"Then she'll just have to wait 'til we get home. I ain't stopping for no bottle."

Iris wailed.

Lily caught her breath.

Quan banged the steering wheel. "Shut that kid up, Lily! You know I can't stand that racket."

"Quan, she's just a baby. She'll be all right when she gets her bottle."

"So, you can see everybody's point but mine, huh? Is that it, Lily?" Quan jabbed at his temples. "You can see yo' nosy mamma's point; yo' point; this here yelping baby's point, but not my point. Oh, I see it now!" Quan made a violent U-turn on Lancaster Road in the middle of rush hour traffic. Horns blared their disapproval. "I see now! It ain't never gonna change!"

"Quan!" Lily was getting really scared. "What're you doing?"

Quan popped open the secret compartment under his custom-built dashboard. He pulled out his chrome-plated .357 Magnum. He propped it on his lap.

"Quan! Please! Where're you going?"

"Hush up, Woman!" Quan yelled. "You'll see." And then he went dead, cold, silent.

Lily could hardly remember how to pray, even though she'd grown up spending every Sunday and Wednesday with her parents at Overcoming Faith Church. Even after her dad died when she was fifteen, her mother, Flora, or Mother Brown to the church folk, insisted they continue to observe the twice weekly services.

Her mother had done her best to train her up right, but it had never been enough for Lily. Her mother's world was just too boring. Lily craved the glamorous life—clothes and cars; grown men and freedom. No lame single's ministry; no sissy-acting church boys for her. She wanted the kind of man who'd *go to the trunk for her*—a man who always demanded respect for himself and for her. She wanted a hero, not a zero. She wanted a rough-neck who knew his way around the fast streets of Oak Cliff, on the south side of Dallas, Texas.

In the post white-flight era of the '60s and '70s, Oak Cliff had been characterized by well-to-do black families, good schools, and better athletes. But when these families set their sights on the more affluent northern-tier suburbs of Plano and Frisco, or southern-tier suburbs like Duncanville and DeSoto, Oak Cliff was in-filled by immigrants and working class folk. Pro football players, famous recording artists, and backyard swimming parties gave way to gang colors, Tejano music, and front-yard barbeques. There was a church on every corner, and the megachurches had been left with their fingers stuck squarely in the dike, trying to hold back the floodwaters of decline.

But in spite of her church upbringing, Lily was speeding down Lancaster Road with Quan, the man of her dreams—head dawg, top thug—who'd beat her without provocation, and whose gun was pointed at her and their baby. Lily closed her eyes and tried to squeeze out a prayer, while muffling Iris' hungry cries.

"We're here!" Quan announced in a freaky, fright-night voice.

Lily opened her eyes. "My church?" she whispered. "Quan, why'd you bring me to Overcoming Faith?"

"'Cause it's time yo' mamma gets to see who's boss."

"What?" Lily didn't want Mother Brown to see her like this. "Quan! No! What're you doing?"

"No?" Quan scowled, strapped on his .357, and snatched Lily by her long, flowing hair. "You don't tell me 'no'."

"Owww!" Lily yelped, as Quan yanked her toward the driver's seat. She managed to ease Iris to the floorboard just as Quan snatched her across the console. The gear shift dug into her thighs with every tug until he finally jerked her through the driver's side door.

"Quan, what're you doing?" Lily's knees buckled when her feet hit the pavement at 401 Bradford Street in South Oak Cliff. But it was like Quan couldn't hear.

About that time, Mother Brown descended the church steps. She was a night nurse at Oak Villa Nursing Home, but she volunteered at the church office on weekday afternoons until 6:00 p.m.

She stopped short when she spotted Quan on that cold November day. He had a gun pressed against her daughter's temple.

"Hey, there, Old-Nosy-Mother-Brown." Quan snarled. "What'cha gotta say now?"

Mother Brown kept quiet and prayed.

"What? Cat got yo' tongue, Old Woman?"

Some of the other staff who had begun to file out of the church froze in their tracks.

"Didn't I tell you, Old Woman?" Quan growled. "Lily is my woman, and if anybody has anything to say about it, it's gonna be me. I have the last word!" He smacked his non-gun toting hand across his chest in the sign of a 'V'. "I'm Quantavis V'montron Scott," he yapped, "and I always have the last word! Is that clear?"

"Yes, son." Mother Brown squeaked out the words.

"Son?" Quan's finger squeezed the trigger once. *Bam!* "Who's yo' son, now?" He squeezed it again. *Bam!*

# CHAPTER 2: COMFORT
# ONE ANOTHER.

*II Corinthians 1:4*

Nearly six months to the day after she'd buried her precious daughter, Mother Brown was sitting across from Pastor John Mayberry's desk at Overcoming Faith Church. She was sixty-plus and as short as she was round, but she wasn't the kind of woman to be taken lightly. In public, she sported a salt-and-pepper wig pulled down tightly around her ears; but in private, she let her wiry gray hair go natural. Her eyes had a contagious sense of wonder, but they were nearly obscured by black-rimmed glasses due to her failing eyesight. The glasses, which nearly covered her face, gave off a comic bookworm effect.

Mother Brown was engaged in a losing battle with her ten-month-old granddaughter, Iris, who was pretty in a yellow jumpsuit with matching berets holding down the edges of her fluffy curls. Iris was learning to walk and sitting still was not on her menu.

Pastor Mayberry smiled at the pair of them. He was fifty-plus with Obama-like qualities—good and gracious and…*good-gracious!* At least, that was the rep he held with most of the women in the congregation. It was for that reason he rarely granted closed-door meetings with the opposite sex. But this was different. This was Mother Brown, and Mother Brown was a friend.

"I'm so glad to see you, Mother Brown." Pastor Mayberry greeted.

"It's good to be seen, Pastor—"

"And not viewed." The compassionate pastor completed her wisecrack, and they shared a chuckle. It was something her late husband, Deacon Brown, often said. "Mother Brown, we're so glad you took the time to grieve and rest-up before trying to come back to your duties here at the church."

"I don't know how much rest I've been getting." Mother Brown glimmered. "This granddaughter of mine is a busy little handful. She keeps me on my toes. In fact, I think the Lord left her here for just that purpose." She kissed Iris' rosy cheek, and the baby promptly rubbed it off with the back of her chubby little hand in an effort to get down.

"I'm just glad you're feeling up to coming back where you belong." Pastor Mayberry added.

"I would've been back sooner," Mother Brown said, "but I've been in a bad way...2006 was a bad year for me...seeing my Lily killed like that...right before my eyes." She raised her right hand to heaven. "If it hadn't been for Jesus, I tell you, Pastor, I would've lost my mind—"

"I understand." Pastor Mayberry consoled. "Such a tragic loss, and right here at the church's front door. Two, twenty-year-old kids…Murder. Suicide. My Lord!"

"And that's my other cross to bear." Mother Brown admitted. "As hateful of an act as it was, that boy's mother lost her son that day, too. I've had to find it in my heart to forgive him and to reach out to her."

"It's at times like these our faith really makes the difference."

"It wasn't easy, Pastor." Mother Brown clutched Iris close to her breast. "I'm just thankful this baby didn't witness it…her mother saw to that…and she's too young to remember."

"And, prayerfully, with time, it'll get easier for you, too, Mother Brown. Although I know you'll never forget—"

"No. I will *never* forget." Mother Brown gave in and sat Iris on the floor. "In fact, Pastor, I don't ever want to forget." She kept a close eye on Iris as she pulled up on his desk.

"What do you mean?"

Mother Brown wiped the steamy tears off her glasses and steadied her voice. "I loved my daughter, Lily, but she did have her faults—"

"Don't we all?"

"And the main one was her thinking she *had* to have a man." Mother Brown huffed. "Lily wasn't willing to wait and do it the Lord's way. She thought she needed a man to take care of her, and that was that."

"That seems to be a struggle with many of our young ladies." Pastor Mayberry agreed.

"And after going through this, Pastor, that's something I want to address, if you'll let me."

"Go on."

"It occurred to me during this awful time that these young ladies don't so much want a man as they want what a man has to offer."

"Hmm?"

"They need a man to fix their car, or pay a light bill, or give them some attention, or whatever, so they give up their bodies for the services he can provide." Mother Brown explained.

"And he gets what he wants."

"Yep. Sex."

"But from what I'm hearing, young girls today say they want…need sex, too." Pastor Mayberry countered.

"And if that's true, that's between them and the Lord." Mother Brown shrugged. "But what I'm saying is I don't want our young ladies to feel they have to give up their bodies to get the services of a man. They don't have to fall for some…some *wolf.* They can get what they need right here at the church."

"But how would it work?"

"We could start up a new single's ministry for our young ladies." Mother Brown reset her glasses. "They would support one another and help one another with the things they need."

"For example?"

"Let's just say one young lady has a child and another needs a ride to work. Then they could exchange childcare for carpooling."

"Oh, I see." Pastor Mayberry nodded.

"We could even start an Investment Club where every member paid in a little each month." Mother Brown elaborated. "Then if anyone needed to borrow enough to pay a bill or help with some emergency, then they could pay the Club back over time."

"Now, that's an idea."

"Yep, it'll be better for them than going to some high-interest rent-to-own store, or some title loan rip-off joint…or asking some man who just wants to get in their pants—"

"Mother Brown!"

"Pastor, I'm just keeping it real." Mother Brown slowed. "That's why me and my daughter could never see eye-to-eye. I called it like I saw it, and she liked fairy tales; always trying to see more in people than what was there."

"And you want our young ladies to make good choices when it comes to men."

"Yes."

Pastor Mayberry picked up Iris who was pulling up on his pants leg. "How would you organize?"

"We'd meet on a weekly basis at first." Mother Brown floated her idea. "We'd have a short Bible study and then the ladies could discuss their needs and how we could fulfill them. Of course, we'll exchange phone numbers and addresses so we can keep in touch with each other between meetings."

"Sounds good." Pastor Mayberry nodded. "Have you picked a name for the group?"

"Sure have."

"Let's hear it."

"W.O.O.F."

"Woof?" The pastor's fine forehead creased. "Why, that's some name."

"It stands for Women of Overcoming Faith." Mother Brown beamed. "Want to hear our motto?"

"Sure thing."

"'W.O.O.F.—Overcoming the *Wolf*,'" Mother Brown recited. "Get it? We'll be keeping the *wolf* at the door through service and celibacy."

"Okay, it's catchy enough. It might work—"

"It will work, Pastor; you'll see. Young ladies want an alternative to this pay-by-sex nonsense. They just don't know it yet."

Pastor Mayberry caressed Iris' cheek. "And this celibacy thing, how will you make that work?"

"It's in the Bible." Mother Brown giggled. "Besides, I'll be...*the door!*"

"*The door?*"

"Yes, Pastor." Mother Brown peered at him over her glasses. "That's why celibacy doesn't work these days. Parents and adults don't get involved. What young woman can tell a man 'no' after midnight? Please! Her head will be in her heart and her defenses 'round her ankles—"

"Mother Brown!"

"It's the job of grown folks to keep a level head and call a halt to things before they go too far." Mother Brown winked.

"Like a chaperone?"

"Yes," Mother Brown said. "When one of our young ladies wants to date, they can do it at my house, in my living room. If they go to the movie, they can leave from my house and return to my house." She raised her chest and deepened her voice. "And the young man will have to meet...*The Door*...on the very first date."

"*The Door*, huh?" Pastor Mayberry chuckled.

"Yep, I'll help our young ladies decide who goes in and out." Mother Brown winked. "If you know what I mean?"

"Yes, I'm sure I do, Mother Brown." Pastor Mayberry conceded with a smile. "But do you think it'll work?"

"Keep in mind, Pastor, the singles who join this group will want to do it God's way, or else they wouldn't volunteer; right?"

"I see."

"If we can get rid of the *need* factor and the *sex* factor, our young women could be clear-headed enough to pick men for who they are…their character…rather than for what they can do for them."

"Ain't that the truth!"

"Besides, Pastor, I can't figure out why a young woman would want to have sex with a man who doesn't want to marry her…look out for her best interests. Can you?"

"Well, you know, our young men have been damaged by these streets and these bad homes, too," the pastor said. "It's hard for them to truly love themselves let alone a woman."

"True." Mother Brown shrugged. "But there's no reason for them to step-up to be a husband when being a boyfriend can get them all they want?"

Pastor Mayberry nodded. "If you can get the milk for free, why take home a bride—"

"Or a cow!" Mother Brown teased.

The pastor pretended not to notice her humor at his expense. "I'm just amazed you want to take this on," he said. "After the tragedy you've experienced, it's so easy to get bitter—"

"Or you can help others get better."

"You're so right." The pastor nodded. "Tragedy can lead to misery or ministry. It can make you softer toward the leading of God, or more hard-hearted and bitter." He smiled. "I'm so glad you've chosen the better part."

Mother Brown sniffed. "I'd rather be hurt a thousand times, Pastor, than to be bitter once. Jesus paid too high a price to set me free, and it's free I'm gonna be!"

"W.O.O.F. sounds like a good idea, but let's be honest." Pastor Mayberry shifted. "Are you sure you're up to it?"

Mother Brown shook one chunky thigh. "I know I'm short and wide, Pastor, but I'm pretty feisty for an old girl." She bobbed her head like a teenager on headphones. "Matter of fact, I plan to retire and devote myself full-time to this ministry."

"Then how'll you make ends meet?"

"I've got my pension, and I might take on an odd job or two." Mother Brown confided. "Plus, I had an insurance policy on my daughter. I'll use it for her daughter, now."

"I see you've thought this out." Pastor Mayberry hugged little Iris.

"I've prayed it out." Mother Brown reached for her fidgety granddaughter. "Besides, I've got real motivation."

"And what's that?" Pastor Mayberry sighed, keenly aware his friend was always one step ahead.

"The group will give me a built-in pool of babysitters for my little granddaughter, here." The two of them shared a laugh. "So—" Mother Brown pressed on. "I'll give the appeal for members to the announcing clerk on Sunday, and we can get the group started right away—"

"Hold on, Mother Brown." Pastor Mayberry raised his caring hands in near surrender. "I know you're excited about this, but we need to run this through the deacon over Ministries and Outreach, Deacon Bliss."

"Uh-huh." Flora Brown's eyebrows spiked. She didn't know if the pastor knew it or not, but his wife, Evangelist Johnesther Mayberry and Deacon Raython Bliss were as thick as thieves, and one never knew what kind of reception one would receive from either of them. It seemed to depend on how the idea fit into their megachurch scheme, which evidently was known only by the two of them, and certainly too grand to share with the rest of the measly 200 members of Overcoming Faith, including the pastor.

More than once, Mother Brown had overheard the whispers from the senior women concerning Evangelist Mayberry: "She don't seem to care nothing 'bout us;" or "It feel like she just practicing on us." Not to mention Deacon Bliss and his flirty ways. But Mother Brown had her ear to the ground and her bifocals firmly fixed on that pair. They couldn't pull the wool over her eyes.

"I'll have Deacon Bliss contact you," Pastor Mayberry continued, "and y'all can decide about the ministry charter, meeting times, and the like, and then the announcement can be made to solicit members."

"Sure thing, Pastor; whatever you say." Mother Brown relented. "But I see this as critical, and I don't want us to drag our feet."

"I do understand." Pastor Mayberry smiled, delighted that the Lord had traded her pain for purpose. Seeing light in the eyes he'd given up for dead just six months ago over at Overcoming Faith Cemetery was its own reward. "Trust me, Mother Brown." The pastor agreed. "We'll get right on it."

# CHAPTER 3: PREFER
# ONE ANOTHER.

*Romans 12:10*

Deacon Raython Bliss was a strapping hunk of a man covered in a dark chocolate wrapper. He was an ex-college football hero who never quite made it in the pros. Now, on the tail-end of forty, he was graying nicely at the temples, clean shaven and fine. Most days, he wore gold-tipped cowboy boots and a black felt ten-gallon hat. Over the years, he'd practiced his *I'm-just-a-good-ole-country-boy-from-East-Texas* drawl to a disarmingly sexy perfection.

He had also become a very shrewd and successful businessman along the way. He owned both a commercial janitorial service and a moving business, which he operated out of a warehouse in the Redbird Airport Industrial Complex. In their small congregation, he doubled as the Finance Director. He was married to Marvella, who constantly struggled with her weight, but whose sweet and supportive disposition was worth its weight in gold. However, they had no children to show for their twenty-five-plus-year union.

"Well, hello-there, Mother Brown," Deacon Bliss crooned over the telephone in his church office. A pair of longhorns graced the walls and a cowhide rug gave it that homey touch. "Ray Bliss, here, at yo' service." He reared back in his black, tooled-leather chair and planted his boots squarely on his desktop.

"Hello, Deacon." Mother Brown inserted. "How's Sis. Marvella?"

"Marvella? She be fine. Thank y'all for asking." Deacon Bliss was quick to flip the script. "But I'm calling 'cause Pastor says you wanna start up some sort o' new group for the little, single fillies at our church."

"Actually, it's a single's ministry for our young ladies." Mother Brown corrected. "And, yes, we'd like to get underway as soon as possible."

"Now, hold yo' horses there, Mother. Give this ole boy a chance to wrap his mind around y'all's idea."

"I'm sorry, Deacon Bliss, I thought Pastor Mayberry had brought you up to speed."

"Well, he has; he did. But I just wanna be sure it'll be good for our church and won't cause no outlandish strain on the budget."

"I see."

"Do you have y'all's budget set out yet?"

"Well, our budget will be minimal. The young ladies will support each other in ways that won't cost the congregation as a whole." Mother Brown explained.

"Good. Good."

"I've drafted a charter for your review—"

"Just get it over to my secretary, and I'll get back with you when I'm satisfied." The deacon rumbled. "In the meantime, if y'all's budget is gonna to be less than $1,000 a year, I guess it wouldn't hurt for y'all to go ahead and move forward—"

"Thanks for your approval, Deacon Bliss."

"Approval? Did I say I was approving the thing? I'm just letting you move forward to see what kind of interest you'll get from the…young ladies in our congregation."

"I'll prepare the announcement for first Sunday." Mother Brown offered.

"Okay. We'll wiggle the bait and see who bites." Deacon Bliss' voice warmed. "How's that pretty, little granddaughter of yours; Iris; ain't it?"

"Yes, it's Iris; and she's fine." Mother Brown clipped. "Thank you for asking. Goodbye."

"So, what did she say, Bliss?" Evangelist Johnesther Mayberry nudged. She'd been hanging on his elbow throughout the entire conversation.

Evangelist Mayberry was the pastor's wife and an ordained minister. And although she was a gorgeous woman, whose dazzling teeth and made-to-order smile set her apart, she'd taken on the title to distance herself from the other women in the congregation. She was thick in all the right places, and when she chose to sit in the pulpit, she usually covered her curvaceous legs with a dyed-to-match hankie so as not to be a distraction to the deacon's corner. But she was forty-nine going on fifty and trying to escape the gnawing feeling that she was running out of time to achieve the goals she'd set for herself.

"You heard," Deacon Bliss responded. "It's just some bee Mother Brown's got stuck in her bonnet."

"Yes, since she did such a poor job of raising her only child, I guess she's trying to raise everybody's daughter, now; huh?" Johnesther sniped.

"Sort o' makes me happy me and Marvella never had no kids—"

"Yeah, I've always wondered how that went down." Johnesther jeered. "Was it you or her that couldn't—"

"Must o' been her." Bliss' boots hit the floor. "All my pipes is working a hundred-and-one percent. Wanna see?" He stood up to unfasten his big, shiny belt buckle.

"Dream on, Ray Bliss." Johnesther raised her hand to stop his progress. "I don't need that kind of drama."

"Chicken!" The deacon chuckled and returned to his chair. "Speaking of children, where's y'all's only son these days?"

"Off saving the world in Alaska...somewhere. You know he's a botanist, and they're testing global warming, or some such nonsense, up there in all that cold."

"Do you ever think about the baby you lost?"

"Of course not, Bliss!" Johnesther shot him a face-full of daggers. "Why would you dredge up that old news?" She flopped into a nearby chair. "That was over ten years ago, and you know I'm over it. In fact, I'm rather glad we only had the one son, and that he's grown and gone. I need to focus on the needs of this church!"

"Yeah, I know. And that's why I made sure Flora Brown won't strain the church's budget none." Deacon Bliss chuckled wickedly. "The idea will probably flop like a cow's tit anyhow. I can't see these fast-tail gals being down for no *celibacy* club."

"You're right about that." Johnesther crossed her shapely calves. "But somebody's got to protect my husband from all the hair-brained schemes these folks come up with." She flashed him a glossy smile. "I guess that would be us."

"It sure ain't Sensay—"

"Absolutely not!" Johnesther pursed her ruby lips. "Our esteemed Assistant Pastor Sensay Logan has few dreams and even less vision where this church is concerned."

"You got that right!"

"Sensay thinks church is all about preaching and soul saving." Evangelist Mayberry frowned. "But church is about growth, and one day my husband will see it if we can keep these lunatics from blocking his vision."

Ray Bliss clucked his tongue. "You've got a real fine mind for a cute little filly."

"Make no mistake, Bliss. I'm nobody's *filly*." Evangelist Mayberry bristled. "I was named for my shotgun-toting daddy and Queen Esther, and that means I take bunk off o' no man, including you."

# CHAPTER 4: BE SUBJECT TO
# ONE ANOTHER.

*1 Peter 5:5*

"Good morning, Church." The announcing clerk waddled to the podium at Overcoming Faith on the first Sunday in May. "These are your announcements for the week: All mothers and daughters are invited to attend the Annual Mother's Day Tea to be held Saturday before the second Sunday in May at 4 o'clock p.m. in the Fellowship Hall. Next, the Silver Stars are inviting all seniors over sixty-five to their Annual Picnic to be held on the Friday before the fourth Sunday at noon in Kiest Park. Those planning to attend, please contact Evangelist Mayberry or Sis. Blanchard."

She turned the page. "Mother Brown would like to meet with all young, single women this Friday night at 6 o'clock p.m. in the Fellowship Hall in order to start up a new single's ministry, which will provide fellowship, support, and spiritual growth. The name of the new group is W.O.O.F." The short, chunky clerk snickered. "That is…Women of Overcoming Faith."

The congregation rustled with interested smiles, but Johnesther Mayberry's ears locked up tight. Her lips drew into a thin line. Her eyes dotted like periods behind a short sentence. She was so angry she didn't mind that her aqua blue hankie, a perfect match to her fine tailored suit, slid to the floor of the pulpit. She didn't even bother to pick it up. She didn't care if the sight of her brown-sugar legs upset the Deacon Board. Following that bombshell of an announcement, she couldn't make heads or tails of her husband's sermon either, and she didn't pretend to. She'd have it out with him as soon as they got home.

****

Evangelist Mayberry's jaws were tight all the way home on the ride from church. They lived in Shady Oaks Manor, a subdivision of 4,000 square foot homes, rolling hills and mature trees in the Redbird section of Oak Cliff. She'd decided to wait until Pastor Mayberry parked their Cadillac Deville in their four-car garage before giving him a piece of her mind. She didn't want him to be able to escape one word she had to say.

"What were you thinking?" Johnesther's tirade began as soon as they hit the kitchen.

"What're you talking about, honey?" Pastor Mayberry laid his keys on the counter.

"What am I talking about?" The evangelist blasted. "Did it ever occur to you to run the name of Flora Brown's group past me?"

"Honey, calm down. I don't understand—"

"You don't understand? That's your problem. You never understand anything!" Johnesther snatched off her pearl and diamond earrings and slammed them on the granite countertop. "Don't you realize, Husband, that with a name like, *Women of Overcoming Faith*, everybody in town will associate it with me; think I'm over it; or think I should be over it; or wonder why I'm not over it!"

"Johnesther, to be honest with you, I never gave the name a second thought—"

"Obviously not!" Johnesther ranted.

"Mother Brown came to me because the Lord laid it on her heart to reach out to young women so they won't end up like her daughter and—"

"And what?" Johnesther said flippantly. "You just lost your mind and let her name it *Women of Overcoming Faith*? I'm the only woman at Overcoming Faith that should be over a ministry carrying that title. I'm the First Lady!"

"But, honey, you're over the Silver Stars and the Senior Women's Ministry." The pastor reasoned. "Why would you begrudge Mother Brown from working with the singles?"

"Begrudge her? I don't begrudge her a thing!" Johnesther sizzled. "I just think the name is highly inappropriate for any woman to bear other than your own wife! Can't you see that?"

"Honey, I thought you'd be glad that something good has come out of Mother Brown' tragedy—"

"Mother Brown's tragedy! Mother Brown's tragedy! I'm so sick of everybody focusing on something that happened nearly a year ago." Johnesther flailed her arms.

"And besides, it's her own fault it happened in the first place—"

"Johnesther!" Pastor Mayberry's handsome face registered his alarm. "How can you say a thing like that?"

"Because it's true!" Johnesther stormed. "If Mother Brown had spent more time minding her own business, rather than meddling in church business, this *tragedy* would've never happened!"

Pastor Mayberry held his ground. "Only the Lord knows why it happened, Johnesther; but I'd think you'd be glad to see something good come of it, for the sake of our young women—"

"And about the name?" Johnesther patted her foot in her designer pumps.

"The name stays!" Pastor Mayberry stripped off his pin-stripped tie and escaped upstairs to his study.

# CHAPTER 5: SPEAK TRUTH TO ONE ANOTHER.

*Ephesians 4:25*

Mother Brown didn't know what to expect at the second meeting of W.O.O.F., but she was laying out plenty of refreshments just in case anybody showed up. The first meeting, held on the previous Friday night, had been lively to say the least; over thirty young, single women showed up. However, the group had gotten off to a rocky start when Mother Brown hit them with this gem: "If we want to be blessed, we've got to serve one another."

*Huh?*

"And in this group," Mother Brown went on to say, "we're going to take real good care of each other by keeping our focus on the *'one-another'* scriptures in the Bible."

Then a young lady on the front row raised her hand, and things got downright heated. "But Mother Brown," she said, popping her gum in rhythm, "what's this celibacy thing I heard about?"

Mother Brown met her question head on. "It means, my sister, as Christian women we commit to living the Lord's way. We commit to waiting until we're married to have sex—"

"What?" Her rebuttal trailed off. "But I'm just saying—"

Another timid soul raised her hand in the back of the room. "Is it in the Bible...about us not having sex before marriage?"

"Yes." Mother Brown assured her. "Does anyone have their Bible handy?"

Two young women eased up their hands.

"Will one of you read, I Thessalonians, Chapter 4, verse 3?" Mother Brown instructed. "And all of us can read the entire chapter when we get home."

A pretty brown woman with dreads, glasses, and the faint aroma of incense stood and read eloquently. "For this is the will of God, even your sanctification, that you should abstain from...fornication." Quietly, she took her seat. You could hear a mouse peeing on cotton.

Suddenly, a prophetic voice swelled up from the rear of the room. "But nobody practices that teaching anymore!"

Then opinions started whizzing around the room like ping pong balls.

"And just maybe that's why we're in this mess—"

"Yeah, babies having babies—"

"Yeah, babies killing babies—"

"Women getting AIDS—"

"And ole nasty STDs—"

"Beat down by their low-life man—"

"Tricked out by their no-good—"

"But y'all!" One brave soul shouted. "Don't we need sex?"

"I know I do!"

"Me, too!"

"Okay, ladies." Mother Brown reeled them in, trying to stave off a mass stampede for the exits. "I don't want you leaving here tonight thinking God is against sex," she said. "God wants us to have sex…with our husbands. He wants us to have strong families and babies…with our husbands."

Just then a cute little boy dressed in bibbed overalls let out a happy squeal, and his mother shushed him.

"Amen!" Mother Brown smiled, and the group released a tense chuckle. "You see, God doesn't want us women out here alone fending for ourselves and our children. He wants us to wait until we're married to have sex," she said, "for our own protection."

"Protection? What protection?" a voice blared from the middle of the room.

"In a loving relationship, our husbands are to cover us…like Christ does the church," Mother Brown replied, "and give us physical protection, financial protection, emotional protection—"

"Yeah, right!" an anonymous voice scorned, and the room buckled back down under a mass of murmurs.

"I understand what you mean." Mother Brown quieted the group. "We all know of situations where husbands don't do their part, but that's why the Lord wants us to marry men that follow after Him."

"But it's hard to find a good man!" A slim woman worked her neck.

"You're right about that, and that's why the Lord wants us to wait until we're married for sex, so we don't get burdened down with bad relationships, diseases, unwanted pregnancies...or worse." A lump caught in Mother Brown's throat when she thought of her precious daughter, Lily, lying dead in the street. "The Lord loves us, ladies." She sighed. "But for the Christian life to work in our favor, we have to do it His way."

Following such a spirited debate and the dubious parting looks from the ladies, Mother Brown didn't know how many, if any, would return to the second meeting; but she was about to find out. They had decided to meet on Wednesday nights, rather than Fridays, in keeping with Overcoming Faith tradition. The church was a beehive of activity on Wednesday nights, filled with Bible studies, small group meetings, choir practices, business meetings, and W.O.O.F wanted to be part of the action. This was also the night they were to elect officers and move forward.

Happily, a few young ladies began to file into the Fellowship Hall and take a seat—six total. All but two of them sat in separate parts of the room, as far away from each other as possible. It almost took an Act of Congress for Mother Brown to persuade them to sit closer together in the front of the room.

"Well, it's six o'clock, ladies," Mother Brown greeted, "so I guess we'd better get started. We want to always be respectful of your time." She clasped her hands together. "I'm so glad you're here. I was beginning to think I'd have to eat all this queso dip by myself."

That comment earned at least a smile from the group. Mother Brown was full of life, but even the thought of her adding another pound to her short, round frame was not a pretty one.

"I tell you what," Mother Brown said, "let's just take a few minutes and introduce ourselves." She felt the tension thickening again. "And so as not to put anyone on the spot, I'll go first; okay?"

"Okay."

Mother Brown gave them her name, rank and serial number. She also filled them in on the death of her daughter and introduced them to her precious little Iris, stationed in her playpen. Her rosy face and stingy-toothed grin were the best ice-breaker yet.

The lady with the red hair, piled high, and long, multi-colored nails chimed in next. "Hi, I'm Laqueeta Lee, 30-something." The gold on her front tooth gleamed when she smiled. She had a short, tight body, which she swiveled around in her figure-hugging jeans to tell them she was a dental assistant and her hobby was reading.

"And I'm proud to say I have two pre-teen boys, Mack and Mike, and they keep me plenty busy."

But what she didn't tell them was that her sons had two different dads. And the reason they exhibited such bitter sibling rivalry was because she had too many boyfriends to take the time to talk to them about being a loving and accepting family unit. Nor did she tell them her real hobby was taking advantage of trusting people and easy pickings—getting something for nothing was her game. What she said was, "I want to join this group 'cause it'll help me read my Bible more." *Ting!*

Next up was Angel Rojas, 20. She was nearly six feet tall, thin and lanky, wearing a blue and gold team jogging suit. Her coal black hair was pulled back into a tight bun, the kind serious athletes wear to sharpen their vision, and she didn't fool around with makeup. She explained that she'd grown up at Overcoming Faith, and her mom and dad were still members. She was a junior at nearby Denton College on a volleyball scholarship. "I obey the rules," Angel said with the pride of a premiere athlete, but with a lack of love in her voice. "I want to be part of this group because I believe in my church."

But what she didn't say was she was her parent's only child, and they had very high expectations of her, even though she didn't feel like she fit in anywhere—not in the Hispanic world, or the Black world, and certainly not on the White campus. She refused to speak Spanish. She didn't have any boyfriends and no prospects, so it didn't matter where she spent her evenings. It might as well be at Overcoming Faith.

"Rojas?" Laqueeta frowned. "I'm just saying...you look a little Hispanic, but you talk like a sistah." She plied the room for confirmation. "Don't she, y'all?"

"Angel's voice dropped to a whisper. "My dad is Hispanic. My mom's Black."

"Ohhh! See! I told y'all—"

Mother Brown stepped in right on time to deflect the brouhaha. "And what's your name young lady?" she said.

All eyes turned to the petite girl sitting next to Angel. They had come in together and sat together from the beginning. "Who me?" She finally looked up from texting on her chrome cell phone. Having crash-landed from cyberspace, she peered at them as if they were little green Martians. "I'm just here with Angel...really." She tilted her head to one side. "And I'm so totally *not* joining this group."

"But since you're here," Mother Brown said, "please introduce yourself."

She was a gorgeous blonde with crystal blue eyes and straight, white teeth. If she wasn't sitting there at Overcoming Faith, she could've been on a fashion runway in Paris. "Okay. I'm Gabbi...Gabbi Prentiss, 20." She twirled one of her long blonde curls. "So, my given name is really Gabriella, but *everybody* calls me Gabbi." She told them she was Angel's roommate and a cheerleader at Denton College. Her parents lived in nearby North

Richland Hills, but she didn't see them very often. "See, I'm only here because Angel needed a ride, and I've got the car." She giggled like the blonde cheerleader she was.

But what she didn't tell them was her parents were filthy rich and spoiled, and they didn't have time for her. They never had time for her. Angel was her only female friend. All the other girls on campus hated her because the entire football team *knew* her in a biblical sense.

Next up was Rachael Jones, 25, and her son, Jake, age 5. Rachael had liquid brown skin, big-screen eyes, no makeup, and nails chewed down to the quick. Her thick, dark hair was crawling out of its rubber band. She wore jeans and a sweat shirt and constantly fingered a fine gold locket that looked out of place around her neck. As it turned out, Jake was the little boy in the bibbed overalls from the first meeting. Rachael said she was a college drop-out, but she was making every effort to re-enroll. She admitted she'd made some mistakes, "But I want to do better now. I want to make a good life for Jake and me."

But what she didn't tell them was her mother was dead, and she never knew her dad. She and little Jake were barely hanging on with food stamps, odd jobs, and an occasional hand-out from Jake's dad. And of late, they were sleeping nights in her beat-up, old station wagon just to survive.

With some prompting, Choice King, 29, spoke-up. She was the type that didn't talk unless she had something important to say. She barely lifted her head, but when she spoke, the rich melody in her voice was hauntingly beautiful and overwhelmingly sincere. "I'm here," she said, "because I need your prayers." She told them she'd been through a lot, but she wasn't prepared to go into it, "Until I know we're family."

But what she didn't tell them was she was a recovering drug addict. One night, when she'd been sliding down the stall of a public toilet, passing out from a drug overdose, she saw the words, "Jesus Saves," knifed into the wall. In her haze, she cried out, "If you're really there, Jesus, save me!" And He did. She'd done her stint in rehab, and she'd found herself a steady job at a florist on Zang in Oak Cliff. Now, she'd come to Overcoming Faith to rebuild her life.

Iris whined, and Choice rescued her from the playpen.

"Well, I guess I'm last." Fancy Chambers flung back her pricey bronze extensions. She said she was 24, a college graduate with a promising career as a paralegal at Lark & Lawson, a respected law firm in Plano, a north Dallas suburb. She looked the part in a gray business suit and sterling silver accessories. She'd passed the LSAT exam and she'd been accepted into SMU Law School for the fall. "Go Mustangs!"

But what she didn't tell them was that she and her two brothers grew up homeless with their psycho mother who'd been unable to hold down a job. So, after they'd worn out their welcome with relatives and friends, they'd lived in their mom's bombed-out car for much of her childhood. As the eldest, Fancy basically raised her two brothers, but she'd done well in school. She had to. She joined every club imaginable to keep from going back to that car in that alley until the last possible moment. She hoarded all the food she could find at school in order to feed her brothers. She would even sneak back to the gym early mornings to shower and change to keep her classmates in the dark. A well-deserved college scholarship had freed her from that life, and she despised every reminder of it. She didn't care what Evangelist Mayberry wanted; she wasn't about to let these "*little W.O.O.F. people*" invade her life.

\*\*\*\*

Without Mother Brown's knowledge, Johnesther Mayberry had made time in her busy schedule, prior to the second W.O.O.F meeting, to woo Fancy Chambers into her camp.

"Hello, my dear." The evangelist had offered Fancy a seat at the grand mahogany desk that presided over her church office. "It's so good of you to come."

"Oh, Evangelist Mayberry," Fancy oozed, "I'm so honored to be invited."

"Think nothing of it, my dear. I know you've been a loyal member of Overcoming Faith for quite a few years now, and I just see this meeting as overdue." The evangelist gave her a glossy smile. She'd noticed this young lady all right because she was pretty and perky, and she'd pegged her as a *climber*. And that was fine, of course, as long as Fancy stayed away from her husband, and she could find somehow to put her social aspirations to good use.

"Well, thank you," Fancy said, wedging more comfortably into her seat. *She's right, of course; it is about time. I pay my tithes. This meeting is well overdue!*

Evangelist Mayberry preened in her high-backed velvet chair. Queen Victoria could've done no less. "My dear, I understand you attended the first meeting of W.O.O.F."

"Yes, I did, but I don't plan to go back."

"And why's that?" the evangelist cooed.

"It's just not for me. I don't need a bunch of women looking over my shoulder, judging my decisions. I'm quite capable of reading and following my Bible on my own."

"I see."

"Besides, I don't play around in the bone yard—"

"Bone yard?"

"Yeah, you know, raking around in my past." Fancy shifted. "That's a lot of psycho-babble nonsense. Life is about here and now…and, of course, the future."

"That's a very interesting perspective, and I do respect it." Johnesther slowed for effect. "It's just that—"

"What?" Fancy leaned forward, as if on cue.

"It's just that the Pastor and I can't be everywhere at the same time; although, of course, we'd love to be."

"But, of course," Fancy said, sizing her up.

"So, I was just thinking…an intelligent woman, such as yourself, could be of great value to us in W.O.O.F."

"Whatever do you mean?" Fancy pressed, tiring of her cat-and-mouse game.

"What I'm saying, dear, is that if you were to become a charter member of W.O.O.F., you could be the eyes and ears for me and the Pastor." Johnesther curled her mouth just so. "Keep us informed, you know."

"Oh," Fancy said, "I see. That could be a very important service to Pastor—"

"Yes." Evangelist Mayberry clipped her gloating short. "And, of course, I would be delighted to take you to lunch, from time to time, to discuss your impressions…say at the Renaissance Hotel."

The mere mention of the Renaissance sent Fancy into hives. She was so excited. "Of course, I'd love to have lunch with you, anytime, anywhere." *Oh, that new pin-striped Armani suit I bought on sale at Marshall's and my Gucci pumps will look divine at the Renaissance. All eyes will be on me!*

"Well, once you've settled into the group," Evangelist Mayberry said, yanking her to a speedy landing, "I'll have my receptionist set something up. Is that all right with you?"

"Perfect!" Fancy rubbed her sweaty palms together. "Perfect!"

****

Mother Brown stood to conclude the second meeting. "Ladies, we're now the seven charter members of W.O.O.F.," she said warmly. "We'll be 'keeping the *wolf* at the door through service and celibacy'. And I think we've accomplished quite a lot tonight. Don't you?" She punctuated her closer with a warm smile. "Tell you what, let's just provide our contact information on the sign-in sheet, include your cell and e-mail, and we'll wait until next time to elect our officers. Is that okay with everyone?"

"Sure."

It was over. The ladies breathed a sigh of relief. A few of them exchanged guarded glances.

"Now, don't any of you even think of leaving here without eating some of this queso." Mother Brown winked.

They loosened up a little and crowded around the refreshment table.

# CHAPTER 6: SERVE
## ONE ANOTHER.

*Galatians 5:13*

Bright and early the next morning, Flora Brown's telephone was ringing off the hook. "Hello, Mother Brown, this is Rachael…from W.O.O.F. I hope I'm not disturbing you."

"That's not possible, Rachael. We're all sisters; remember? What's up?" Mother Brown rested the phone on her shoulder and continued to change Iris' poop diaper.

"I need to ask you a big favor."

"Shoot."

"I have an interview Friday." Rachael slowed. "A chance for some steady work at a local market, and I was wondering if you could keep Jake in the morning?" She quickly added, "I'll be back in the afternoon to pick him up. Promise."

"No problem." Mother Brown smiled. "Me and Iris will be here anyway. Can you and Jake come early, in time to have breakfast with us? We're having pancakes."

"Sure. Thank you. I really appreciate this."

"My pleasure." Mother Brown chipped in. "What're you wearing; on your interview, I mean?"

"My best jeans. Why?"

"Just a thought. We'll see y'all here bright and early tomorrow morning; right?"

"Sure thing!" Rachael brightened. "We'll be there. Bye."

Mother Brown propped Iris in the playpen and hit speed dial. "Good morning, Fancy. How're you this fine morning?"

Fancy stared at her cell phone. "Who's this?"

"This is Mother Brown. I know you're at work, so I'll keep it brief."

"Oh, didn't recognize the number," Fancy replied caustically. "Guess I need to program it in."

"That would be helpful." Mother Brown rushed on. "But I called to ask you to lend Rachael an outfit for a job interview?"

"Who?" Fancy queried. "The one with the little boy?"

"You two are about the same size, and she really needs this job." Mother Brown added.

"I bet she does, but—"

"Nothing fancy, Fancy." Mother Brown giggled at her own pun. "Just reach in the back of your closet and bring out one of those fine pantsuits you're not wearing this season."

Fancy blew out of both nostrils. "Okay. I guess. How do I get it to you?"

"Bring it by my house on your way to work tomorrow—"

"I live and work in Plano." Fancy huffed. "My time will not permit me to come all the way to Oak Cliff before work."

"Then bring it to me tonight after work." Mother Brown insisted. "I'll be home."

"Tonight?"

"Thanks, Fancy, and you have a great day." Mother Brown clicked off the call.

**** 

When Rachael and Jake arrived at her house at 6 a.m. Friday morning, Mother Brown was ready for them. Iris was cleaned, dressed and hungry.

"What's this?" Rachael said when Mother Brown handed her the tasteful, gray pantsuit.

"You said this was an important interview; right?"

"Yes, it is."

"Then you need to look your best." Mother Brown reseated her glasses. "Fancy brought this by for you last night."

"Fancy?"

"Yes, one of your W.O.O.F. sisters; remember?"

"I remember all right," Rachael said, "but why would she do a thing like this for me."

"Because she wants to support your efforts to get a good job." Mother Brown chuckled. "Besides, she may need you to do her a favor someday."

"Me? Fat chance." Rachael sparked. "She's made it quite clear; I'm not in her league."

"Hurry, now." Mother Brown cracked eggs into a bowl. "Get dressed so you can eat with us before you go. I put some shoes on the guest bed that might work for you, too. We probably wore the same size before my feet started all this swelling nonsense.

"But—"

"Just try them and tell me what you think." Mother Brown encouraged.

When Rachael entered the guest bedroom, there were fluffy towels and lavender soap on the bed, alongside a shoe box. She couldn't resist. The hot shower felt like heaven against her skin. She and Jake had been washing off in the ladies' restroom at the truck stop across from where they parked to sleep every night. She felt fairly safe there because of the bright lights and constant movement.

Rachael came into the kitchen looking like a dream. The outfit was a perfect match to the shoes, and they fit her perfectly. "What do you think?" She twirled.

"I think you look fabulous and anybody that doesn't hire you today is a fool—"

"Mother Brown!"

"Well, the truth is the light!" Mother Brown smiled. "Now, sit down and eat a bite before you're on your way."

"Thank you." Rachael fidgeted with her gold locket.

"That's a mighty pretty necklace." Mother Brown commented.

"It was my mamma's," Rachael said quietly. "She's gone now."

"And your dad?"

"Never knew him."

After they put the dishes in the sink, Mother Brown hoisted up little Iris, took Jake by the hand, and they walked Rachael to her car. The thing looked like it could barely run, but Mother Brown didn't say a word. However, when she peeked inside the backseat and saw blankets, dirty socks, and hamburger wrappers, she had to speak up. Nobody had to tell her; they were living in that car.

"Rachael, I've got a great idea." Mother Brown eased into it. "Why don't you and Jake spend the night with us tonight?"

"No." Rachael dropped her head. "We couldn't do that."

"But it would help me out a lot. You see, one of my former patients is having surgery in the morning at the crack of dawn, and he doesn't have any family. He asked me to be there with him, but I didn't know what to do with Iris. I can't take her to the hospital—"

"Oh, Mother Brown, if it would help for me to baby-sit tomorrow, we'd be happy to stay the night." Rachael perked up. "Anything to help you after all you've done for me."

"Okay, then it's a deal. You and Jake in the guestroom, and I'll have dinner ready when you get home." They waved as she drove away. "Be safe."

****

On Sunday morning, Mother Brown's cell phone rang right after Sunday School. "Can somebody come get me? My stupid car gave out on Stemmons Freeway. Just up and quit on me!"

Mother Brown moved away from the chatter around her. "Who's this?"

"It's Fancy! I can't believe it. My Jaguar just died in the middle of traffic! I called the tow truck, but I still need a ride."

"Okay, Baby, okay." Mother Brown tried to calm her. "I'll get Rachael to come get you and bring you to church, and we'll get you home. Tell me exactly where you are."

When Rachael arrived, Fancy was standing with the tow truck. "It's about time!" Fancy pouted. "You buy a top-of-the-line sedan and it leaves you stranded in the middle of traffic!" she yelled for the benefit of the tow truck driver.

"Well, hop in." Rachael offered.

Fancy gave Rachael's beat-up ride the once over. "Is this your car?" Fancy scowled. Of course, she wouldn't let it touch her, but Rachael's hoopty reminded her of the old wreck she and her brothers had lived in with their mother.

It had the same smell—musty gym shoes and greasy french fries.

"Yeah." Rachael glared at her over the hood. "But it works. Get in."

Fancy was careful not to get any stains on her steel gray silk suit and matching patent pumps as she nestled into the passenger seat. "I guess, *thank you*, is in order," she clipped, "but I never thought I'd get stranded on the freeway."

"No problem," Rachael said timidly. "I talked to Laqueeta, and she'll take you home after church."

"La-queeta?" Fancy's lips curled.

"She lives up north, in Richardson; you know—"

"No, I didn't know. I guess I need to look over that sign-in sheet in my inbox." Fancy twirled her eyes. "Is that my pantsuit?"

"It is." Rachael gripped the steering wheel. "I'd planned to return it at our Wednesday W.O.O.F. meeting."

"Don't bother." Fancy scowled. *Does she really think I'd wear that rag after she's had her sorry-behind in it?*

"Gee, thanks," Rachael said, displeased with the *Miss-Lady* attitude she was getting. *It's obvious she's got more money than me, but should that matter? We're both W.O.O.F. members. That should count for something.* "I got the job." Rachael ventured, struggling to keep her cool.

"Good for you." Fancy stared out of the passenger side window.

"I start tomorrow, and we're going to stay with Mother Brown until I get my first paycheck." Rachael elaborated. "She needs help with Iris; you know?"

"Um-hum." Fancy smirked. *I won't bother to ask what kind of job. These homeless women are all alike…stupid, little people with stupid, little lives!*

The long silence in the car was deafening by the time they pulled into the church lot. "Well, we made it," Rachael remarked.

"And none too soon." Fancy bristled.

"I'll put you out here at the front door, and then I'll park—"

With a flick of the door handle, and not so much as a backward glance, Fancy was out of the car and racing up the walkway to the church.

Rachael was left with her mouth hanging open and her engine running hot.

# CHAPTER 7: BE OF ONE MIND TOWARD ONE ANOTHER.

*Romans 12:16*

The next W.O.O.F. meeting began on time with all members present. Since their group was decidedly smaller than expected, they agreed to move their meetings from the Fellowship Hall to a quiet little room just down the hall from the Ministerial Suite, which housed the offices of the pastors, deacons and administrative staff.

"Did anybody remember your assignment?" Mother Brown began.

"What?" They quizzed.

"We were to make a list of the *one-another* scriptures in the Bible—"

"I've been too busy," Angel said.

"No problem." Mother Brown reassured them. "The list is just for our reference anyway."

"Then why does it matter?" Gabbi yawned.

"Because your life is like...a brick house." Mother Brown firmed.

"Brick-house!" Laqueeta broke into the lyrics, swinging her narrow, tear-drop behind to the beat.

Mother Brown's eyes cut her short. "As I was saying," she continued, "if everybody comes along and takes out a brick, how long will you be able to stand?"

"Not long." Rachael supported her position.

Fancy's eyes flashed at Rachael. *Homeless suck-up! She'd agree with anything to keep her free ride going.*

"That's right." Mother Brown nodded. "And other people's lives are that way, too. If we come along and take out a brick and leave nothing in return, it won't be long before they collapse."

"Oh?" Gabbi giggled.

"W.O.O.F. will give each of us an opportunity to give and to get…bricks, if you will." Mother Brown smiled. "Albeit, what we give may not be exactly what we get in return, but we will build each other up and not tear each other down."

"You right," Laqueeta said. "That's what the Lord wants. He wants us to help one another." *Yep, and I'm gonna get all the help I need outta you Bible-thumping suckers. Believe that!*

"So, should we bring the list next week?" Rachael suggested.

"Sure," Mother Brown said, "but we'll add to it as we go along. I think you'll be surprised how many scriptures deal with how we should treat one another."

Choice raised her hand. "I did find a verse on celibacy."

*Oh, no!* Laqueeta curled her lips. *Here we go with that again!*

"Do we want to discuss that tonight?" Mother Brown opened it up to the group.

"Sure; why not?" Angel sighed.

"Then let's have it." Mother Brown smiled.

"I Corinthians 6:18, 'Flee fornication—'"

"Blam!" Mother Brown laughed. "Now, that's a good one; straight, and to the point. And there're lots more. So, do we all agree...the Lord's plan is a good plan?"

"Um-hum," they mumbled.

"No sex before marriage?"

They gave her a disjointed nod.

"Now, what must we do for any good plan to work?"

"I know." Angel recalled from her econ class. "Have a good strategy."

"Right!" Mother Brown exclaimed. "So, what are some strategies to fulfill our plan?"

"Stay away from men," Fancy said under her breath.

"I don't have to worry about that," Angel mumbled, "there're no men in my life."

"Call each other when we need help." Laqueeta added.

"You're absolutely right." Mother Brown seized on the moment. "We can't walk this walk alone. In order to keep the wolf at the door, we're going to need one another, and you're going to need...*the door.*"

"*The Door?*"

"Yes, ladies." Mother Brown peered at them through her thick glasses. "And that would be me. I'm willing to stand between you and the wolf, if you'll let me."

"I don't understand."

"I'll be your chaperone, your mother, your friend, your coach; whatever you need to stay celibate until you marry.

Laqueeta's mouth snapped shut. *Is this old lady for real?*

"Then for sure we've got to pray," Choice said.

"Good idea." Mother Brown agreed. "Let's do that now and at the beginning of each of our meetings." She stood, and they all followed suit. "Choice, since it was your idea, would you lead us in prayer?"

"Me?" Choice gaped.

"Come on, Choice, you can do it," Gabbi cheered.

"Okay, bow your heads everybody," Choice said speedily. "Dear Lord Jesus, we want to live life your way because we know your way is right. Please help us. Amen."

Mother Brown motioned for them to take their seats again. "Well, ladies, I guess we can't put it off any longer. Our charter says we have to elect officers, and tonight's the night."

"We want you to be president, Mother Brown," Rachael spouted.

"No, it should be one of you. I'm just your advisor."

"We trust you, Mother Brown," Angel said.

"And only you." Laqueeta added.

"Okay. Then it's settled." Fancy brought them to closure. "Mother Brown is our president."

"Then you're our vice president." Angel chipped in. She wasn't real fond of Fancy's stuck-up ways, but she was envious of her self-confidence.

"Me?" Fancy pretended not to be flattered.

"Here-here." The ladies voted in unison.

"Okay," Mother Brown continued, "looks like you're our vice president, Fancy. We also need a secretary/treasurer and a chaplain."

"I nominate Rachael as our secretary/treasurer," Angel said, and Fancy's eyes drew down on her like loaded pistols.

"Second." Choice chimed in before Fancy could form her objection.

"Here-here." The group voted, minus one voice.

"And Choice, you've just got to be our chaplain after that sweet, little prayer." Gabbi giggled.

Laqueeta smirked. *That Choice-girl thinks she can read everybody, but I've gotta trick for her. Humph!*

"Here-here." The group voted, minus one voice.

Mother Brown picked up on the building hostility among the women, but she kept it to herself. She simply said, "Women of Overcoming Faith, these are your officers, and we are adjourned."

On the way out, Mother Brown attempted to hug each of them, one by one. "Goodnight, ladies." But the response was generally stiff, and Choice withdrew altogether. *Whew! This is a tough group of women, Lord. So, I guess You want me to love 'em into the Kingdom.*

# CHAPTER 8: CARE FOR
# ONE ANOTHER.

*I Corinthians 12:25*

After the W.O.O.F meeting, Rachael and Jake waited for Mother Brown at the door to the church parking lot. Deacon Raython Bliss stopped by on his way out. "Good evening, my sister." His baritone deepened. He rubbed the crown of Jake's college cut. "You and little man, here, need a ride?"

"No, Deacon Bliss" Rachael fingered her locket. "We're waiting for Mother Brown."

Bliss moved in on Rachael. "Well, if you ever need any little ole thing, Suga, you know who to ask."

Choice made it a point to split them right down the middle on her way out. "Goodnight, Rachael," she said, and deliberately turned her back on the good deacon. Surprisingly enough, Choice was still a virgin, but she'd run into all sorts of ravening wolves while out on the streets. Deacon Raython Bliss was the kind she liked the least—the wolf-in-sheep's-clothing variety.

\*\*\*\*

Rachael's hands tightened on the steering wheel as she drove them home. Jake was dozing in the backseat.

"Mother Brown, can I talk to you about something," she stuttered.

"Sure, Rachael…anything. How's your job going?"

"It's fine. But that's not it."

"What then?"

"It's just that I'm so grateful for you letting me and Jake hangout at your house until I'm able to get my first paycheck—"

"Stop right there!" Mother Brown's voice took on a sharp, playful tone. "People don't *hang out* at my house, young lady. You're family, and my home is your home until you say otherwise."

"I know, and I appreciate it so much," Rachael's voice dipped to a whisper. "It's just that Jake's dad, Tyrone, wants to see him, and I just wasn't sure you'd want him coming around your house."

"Where else would you meet him?"

"We could meet him in the park, like always. It's no problem. It'll be fine."

"You live at my house." Mother Brown countered. "You ought to meet him at my house."

"But I don't want to be a bother—"

"Nonsense. I'm inviting him."

"You are?" Rachael flapped. "You'd do that?"

"Sure. Why not?" Mother Brown's eyes sparkled. "It's about time your wolf came to the door."

"*The door?*" Rachael grinned. "Oh, you mean, you. Okay. Is tomorrow night, right after work, okay?"

"Fine." Mother Brown agreed. "We'll have pizza."

"Yeah, pizza!" Jake squealed from the backseat.

\*\*\*\*

When Rachael put Jake to bed, she found Mother Brown downstairs in the kitchen making a cup of tea.

"Can I tell you something?" Rachael twisted her heart-shaped locket.

"Sure, Baby...anything."

"I think my mamma died of a broken heart."

"Why do you say that?"

"She loved my daddy...whoever he was...but he dumped her before I was even born."

"So, you never knew your daddy?" Mother Brown surmised.

"Nope. My mamma would never confirm or deny she knew who he was either. It drove me crazy!" Rachael quivered. "Whenever I'd ask her, she'd get this strange, faraway look in her eyes and go to a place where I couldn't reach her. Ultimately, I think she died there."

"Does it bother you...not knowing your daddy?"

"Not so much...not anymore, but I don't think Mamma ever got over it." Rachael shuddered. "And when I came up pregnant, it was like pouring salt into an open wound."

"Oh, yes."

"She'd been 19; I was 19. I think the heartbreak of my daddy's betrayal raised its ugly head again and sucked the life right out of her." Rachael slowed. "She never saw her grandson. She died before Jake was born. She was only 38."

"So young."

"Yes. And I swore, even as a little girl, I wouldn't be like my mamma." Rachael teared up. "I promised myself I would never have a baby without being married. I swore to myself!" Her shaky hand traced through her shabby ponytail. "And look at me, Mother Brown. I'm just like my mamma. I can hardly take care of myself or my baby. I'm cursed!"

"But you *are* different from your mom, Rachael."

"How so?" Rachael swiped away the swell of tears.

"You've got Jesus…and me, and W.O.O.F. and all the believers praying for you. You've got hope!"

"That's sure something my mamma never had."

Mother Brown patted her hand. "When Jesus paid for your sins, He broke every curse in your life. Do you believe that?"

Rachael dried her eyes and gave it some serious thought. "Yes," her voice firmed, "I do believe it."

"Then if you believe it, you've got to let it make the difference in your life." Mother Brown smiled a wry smile. "Besides, you've got Tyrone who's at least trying to stay in his son's life. Doesn't that count for something?"

"You're right." Rachael managed a weak smile. "I'm going to bed, now."

"Goodnight, Baby."

****

On Thursday night, at seven o'clock sharp, Tyrone Paige rang the front doorbell.

"I'll get it," Jake screamed, excited to see his dad.

"No, wait, Jake." Rachael cautioned. "Let's look through the peephole first." She opened the door quietly.

"Hey, Rach," Tyrone said.

"Come in."

Tyrone swept Jake up into his arms. "Hey, daddy's little man." Pretty soon they were hugging and tussling, like only boys and their fathers can do.

"Tyrone, I want you to meet Mother Brown," Rachael said.

Mother Brown stood back in her legs and looked him over. "So, you're Jake's dad?"

"Yes, ma'am. Tyrone. Tyrone Paige." He was long, stringy, and looking like a young man with a basketball-jones. He was wearing a wife-beater jersey over sagging jeans so he could show-off his round-ball tattoos.

"Well, have a seat at the dining room table, young man." Mother Brown offered. "We're having pizza."

"Pizza!" Jake cheered, and Iris pulled up on Tyrone's ankle.

He picked her up over his head; and she squealed, loving it. "And who is this pretty, little thing?" He twirled her gently.

"That's my granddaughter, Tyrone," Mother Brown said. "That's Miss Iris."

Tyrone settled her into her highchair and took a seat between Rachael and Jake.

Rachael poked him.

"Oh!" Tyrone rubbed his ribs. "Mother Brown I want to thank you for letting me stop by tonight. I try to see Jake…and Rachael as often as I can."

"We're glad to have you, Tyrone." Mother Brown's eyes gleamed behind her heavy lenses, happily surprised at his manners.

The casual chatter continued until it was time to go. Tyrone was the first to push back from the table. "Well, I've soaked up your hospitality long enough." He smiled. "I'd better get to gettin'."

"It was good to meet you, Tyrone," Mother Brown said. "You live here in Oak Cliff?"

"Yes, ma'am. I live off of Loop 12."

"Then you ought to visit our church some Sundays." Mother Brown winked. "Rachael can tell you how to get there."

Iris started to fidget. She wanted out of her highchair.

"Rachael, get Iris settled in upstairs if you don't mind," Mother Brown said. "I'll walk Tyrone to the door."

"No problem. See you, Ty." Rachael smiled. "Jake, hug your dad goodnight and come on." Jake did as he was told, but it was clear he wanted to hold onto his daddy. He whined and grumbled his way upstairs.

When they got to the door, Mother Brown snatched Tyrone down to her size. "Do you realize your baby and his mother were out on the street?" She buzzed in his ear.

"No ma'am!" Tyrone looked shocked. "I love my son…and Rachael—"

"Young man, love takes care of its own!"

"I want to take care of my son and his mom, but I'm not able right now 'cause I'm living with my parents—"

"And whose fault is that?" Mother Brown rumbled.

Tyrone looked down at her. "But I'm trying to get it together. I'm going to auto mechanic school; I just don't have no money—"

"Then man-up and handle your business, Tyrone."

"Mother Brown?" Tyrone glared, but she didn't flinch.

"Quit hanging with *yo* homeys and playing video games. Finish up your education, get a job, and take care of your family." Mother Brown checked her volume. "You're hurting this child—"

"I'd never do anything to hurt Jake!"

"You don't have to *do* anything to hurt him." Mother Brown squawked. "Not handling your business hurts him!"

"But—"

"And you're going to hate yourself if you don't do right by raising your son, Tyrone. Trust me; I know." Mother Brown slid the door open just wide enough for him to slither out. "Goodnight."

66

# CHAPTER 9: CONSIDER ONE ANOTHER.

*Hebrews 10:24*

"Hi." Rachael smiled at the receptionist who was eating her lunch at her desk on Thursday. "This is the W.O.O.F. Monthly Report for Deacon Bliss."

"But I thought W.O.O.F. was Mother Brown's—"

"I'm the secretary-treasurer."

Bliss' receptionist raised her arched brows. "Oh, I see Miss—"

"Rachael."

"Well, thank you, Rachael. I'll be sure to give it to—"

At that very moment, Deacon Bliss darkened his office door. "Well-well, if it ain't Sis. Rachael...sorry, I didn't catch your last name—"

"Jones."

"Here's her report, Deacon." The receptionist handed it to him, along with a smirk of disapproval.

Bliss grabbed the report from her hand without taking his eyes off Rachael. He stared as though his x-ray vision could see straight through her gauzy summer dress. "Come in, my sister, and let's see what you've got here," he crooned.

"But I'm on my lunch hour—"

"It won't take but a moment." Bliss guided her into his office by her elbow and dumped the unread reports from his guest chair onto the floor. "Have a seat." He pretended to scan her report.

"I hope you find everything in order," Rachael said. "We're new, but we'll get better with time."

"I just bet you will." Bliss sniffed, tail wagging.

"Oh!" Rachael flushed at his double meaning and gathered up her purse to leave.

Deacon Bliss intercepted her at the door. "You don't have to be afraid of me, Suga." He schmoozed. "My bark is *far* worse than my bite."

"All the same," Rachael said, fingering her prized locket, "I've got to get back to work; can't be late."

"Maybe we could talk about your report over lunch next time—my treat." Bliss lowered his voice to a hover. "A young lady such as yo'self, with a child and all, needs all the help she can get. Know what I mean?" He traced his index finger along the bare flesh on her arm.

"Quit that!" Rachael flinched and reached around him to jerk open the door.

Deacon Bliss put on a show for the receptionist. "Well, thank you for stopping by, Sis. Rachael. We'll need to work real close on this thing to get it straightened out." He waved. "Have a blessed day!"

On her way out of Bliss' office, Rachael bumped into Choice in the hallway. "Fancy meeting you here," Choice teased.

"Oh, no! Don't mention that name." Rachael winced. "You know that girl hates my guts."

"Sorry." Choice giggled. "Bad joke."

"No problem. I was just here dropping off our monthly report to Deacon Bliss," Rachael explained, a bit too eagerly.

"And I'm just here to see Assistant Pastor Sensay." Choice returned in kind. "Remember, we voted to invite him to one of our meetings?"

"Oh, yes. Hope he accepts."

"Me, too." Choice wrinkled her nose. "Rachael, are you okay?"

"Sure."

"I know we don't know each other that well, but—"

"But what?" Rachael clipped.

"May I give you a piece of sisterly advice?"

"I guess so, but make it quick." Rachael rustled. "I'm on my lunch hour."

"Men like Deacon Bliss…they don't do to fool with."

"What do you mean?"

"I saw the way he looked at you the other night, and he's a married man." Choice eyed her. "My suggestion…don't ever let that man catch you alone."

Rachael dropped her guard. "Choice, to tell you the truth, I was thinking the same thing."

"Bingo!"

"Girl, you've got a good read on people." Rachael sputtered.

"Let's just say I know my…wolf and wolf-ettes."

"Then maybe you can clear something up for me." Rachael pouted.

"What's that?"

"Why *does* Fancy hate me so? I've never done a thing to that girl."

"Fancy? She doesn't hate you," Choice said. "Fancy hates Fancy."

"But I don't get it. She has everything, and I—"

"But with some folk, if they get a dime more than what they need, they get to thinking they're better than ev-ery-body!"

"Choice-girl, you're a mess." Rachael laughed. "But I guess you're right. We'll have to talk some more, but right now I've got to get back to work."

Choice checked her watch. "Yeah, and I've got to go see Assistant Pastor Sensay."

\*\*\*\*

The members of W.O.O.F. wanted Assistant Pastor Sensay Logan to speak to them—to give them the male perspective on celibacy and the like. The ladies didn't want to embarrass him, but since he was around their age, they figured he could handle it. Besides, as Laqueeta so aptly put it, "I know he kinda young and all, but he a preacher-man; ain't he? He gotta learn to talk about anything to anybody. Well, I'm just sayin'—"

As their newly-elected chaplain, Choice drew the short straw to invite him, and she did so under great duress. She'd never been this close to a preacher before, other than when she'd come down the aisle "to give her hand to Pastor Mayberry and her heart to God." Nonetheless, she'd called ahead to make an appointment during her lunch hour, and she was waiting for the assistant pastor when he arrived.

When Sensay walked through his office door, there stood the prettiest woman he'd ever seen. She took his breath away. But it wasn't just her looks; something about her was calling his name. He couldn't think for the life of him why he'd never noticed her before.

Her head was a mass of natural, raven curls, down to her wavy sideburns. She stood tall and erect; comfortable in her own olive skin. He, on the other hand, was ruddy with a freckled nose and kinky red hair. However, at thirty-two, thick and strong, he was considered handsome in some circles.

"How do you do?" He stretched out his hand to greet her. "I'm Sensay Logan, and I'm told you're the brand-new chaplain of W.O.O.F." His smile faded when she barely shook his hand.

"Choice. Choice King."

"Choice? That's an interesting name—"

"So is Sensay."

"My dad was Christian; my mother Muslim. The marriage only lasted long enough to produce me." The assistant pastor smiled. "And what about you?"

"My mom—my aunt—gave me the name."

"So, which is it?" Sensay quizzed. "Your mom or your aunt—"

"Both. Neither. It's a long story."

"Anyway, have a seat, Sis. King." He sat beside her in the matching guest chair stationed in front of his desk.

"I'm here, Assistant Pastor—"

"Do we have to rush into it?" Sensay tried to ease her obvious tension.

"I just need to get it out before I lose my nerve." Choice said frankly. She still felt a little unworthy when it came to talking to *straight* folk.

"Then get it out, by all means." Sensay smiled. The melody in her voice stirred something warm in his belly.

"We'd like you to come speak at our W.O.O.F meeting, at your earliest convenience." Choice cleared her throat. "We've been studying how to serve one another and—uhh—about…celibacy…and the ladies would like a male perspective."

"But why me?"

"Because…you're about our age and—"

"No matter, Choice; I'd be delighted." The assistant pastor drank in her deep-set, auburn eyes. "But it may be a little while before I can shift things around on my schedule—"

"Great!" Choice hopped up and bolted for the door. "Whenever!"

\*\*\*\*

Meanwhile up in North Dallas, Fancy was making her grand entrance at the classy Sphinx Restaurant in the five-star Renaissance Hotel. She settled in for lunch in one of the white leather chairs stationed at the elegant black table.

"We've only been meeting over a month, now," Fancy said. "There's really not much to report, Evangelist Mayberry."

"Oh, my dear, did I lead you to believe I was bringing you here for a W.O.O.F report? You couldn't be further from the truth. I just wanted us to have a nice chat and a relaxed lunch." Johnesther Mayberry offered her best smile. "What a divine suit, my dear. Where on earth did you find it?"

"It's an Armani" is all Fancy would divulge. She wasn't about to disclose her bargain shopping tips to the likes of Johnesther Mayberry.

"Isn't this a lovely room?" Johnesther mused. "I just adore these enormous floral arrangements."

"Flown in fresh daily."

"Phenomenal."

"Quite."

They ordered.

"So how *are* things with W.O.O.F.?" Johnesther spooned into her luscious crab bisque.

Fancy carefully sifted her words. She had nothing of significance to report, but she didn't want to miss out on another fabulous lunch. "Oh, as fine as can be expected, I guess," she said.

"What on earth do you mean?"

"To tell you the truth, Evangelist, there're only seven of us, including Mother Brown."

"Seven?" Johnesther rested her spoon. "But I thought over thirty young women showed up for the first meeting."

"But by the second meeting, it was down to seven."

"Hardly worth mentioning—"

"But we do have some very lively discussions," Fancy tossed in quickly. "And Assistant Pastor Sensay is going to speak to us very soon."

"What on earth for?"

"The group wants a male perspective on...celibacy."

"Then he's your man!" Johnesther giggled. "He's so awkward around women. I doubt if he's ever seen one naked." They tempered their laughter when heads began to turn at the next table.

"But I don't know how much time I'll have to give the group in the fall." Fancy continued.

"And why's that, my dear?"

"I've been accepted into law school...SMU."

"Really?" Johnesther twinkled.

"Yes, and I plan to fast-track my courses so I can pass the bar before—"

"Before—" Johnesther nudged.

"Before…our new Children's Education Building is under construction."

"Oh?" Johnesther's jaw dropped. "Why's that?"

"Well, it may require me to work two jobs and overtime, but my plan is to be available to head-up our church's legal team in time for the construction phase."

Johnesther twisted her brows. "Is that so?"

Fancy pressed on. "I don't mean to be presumptuous, Evangelist, but one has to set goals; doesn't one?"

"But, of course, my dear." Johnesther regained her composure. "And I'm sure special congratulations are in order. Let's get the maître d' and order some sinful dessert; shall we? And I'll be sure to keep your legal aspirations in mind as we expand our church."

*Mission accomplished!* Fancy dipped into her decadent, crème brûlée. *I don't owe those little W.O.O.F. women one, solitary thing. I have my own career to consider!*

# CHAPTER 10: EXHORT
## ONE ANOTHER.

*Hebrews 3:13*

The seasons had changed by the time the assistant pastor was able to clear his calendar to meet with W.O.O.F. The chill of fall had begun to fill the night air. "Good evening, ladies. I'm Sensay Logan, and it's a pleasure to be with you tonight." His relaxed manner was matched by his black, cable knit sweater.

"Good evening." They chimed politely.

*I guess he a'ight, if you like latte.* Laqueeta sized him up. *But as for me, myself, I like my coffee black.*

Angel was in the midst of waging war with her drooping eyelids. She was dog tired from her afternoon workout in the weight room, and sleep was calling her name.

In the back row, Fancy was rubbing a nervous hand through her braids. It was 6 p.m., and she had an overdue paper which had to be in her law professor's hands no later than 7 p.m., sharp. Covertly, she was submitting it over her hand-held device, and the weak internet connection in the meeting room was giving her fits.

"I know our time is limited, so let's get right to it." Sensay smiled over the group from the podium. "Can someone give us a definition for sin?"

Rachael's hand popped up. She was eager to share what she'd recently learned in Bible study. "Sin is anything we do, think, or feel that doesn't please God."

"Good answer." Sensay smiled. "So based on that definition, Romans 3:23 is right: 'We all have sinned and come short of the glory of God.'" He glimmered. "Truth be told, in one way or another, we sin every day. Am I right?"

The women giggled nervously.

"I say that at the outset, ladies, because I want you to know I'm not here to condemn anyone." Sensay's face was warm and sincere. "The Bible is God's love letter to each of us, and He makes us a wonderful promise in I John 1:9: 'If we confess our sins, He is faithful and just to forgive us our sins and to cleanse us from *all* unrighteousness.' And that's real good news; right?"

The women nodded to the extent they were listening.

Nonetheless, Sensay pressed on. "I delayed my coming to you until now because I wanted you to have the benefit of a very valuable conference I attended this summer," he said. "So tonight, in keeping with your on-going theme of service and celibacy, we're going to discuss: 'The Impacts of Single-Parent Homes on Children'." He rested on the podium. "Because if we have sex outside of marriage, odds are we'll be creating a single-parent home. Amen?" His warm, hazel eyes pleaded for their attention.

"Okay-then!" Laqueeta popped off. "It's about time a man came up in here and told us why y'all don't take care o' y'all's kids!"

"Or why men treat *good* women so bad." Rachael spouted without thinking. She tried to cover her untimely remark with a smile, but it had the look of pain in it.

"Whoa!" Sensay raised his hands. "If we want to go there, I'm sure there's plenty of blame to go around."

"Well, ladies, he could be right." Laqueeta wiggled around in her calfskin jeans. "I guess it ain't all about the brothas. We do be bringing our own—"

Mother Brown's stern eye made Laqueeta rethink her next choice of words in front of the clergyman.

"I'm just sayin'—" Laqueeta backed off. "We do be bringing our own...*hell-o*...up in here."

"You're so right, my sister." Sensay conceded, determined to move on. "And that sounds like a good topic for another time. But on tonight, we want to discuss the self-esteem issues that can arise in both boys and girls when the dad is not in the home, and the intense sibling rivalry that can occur when the children in a home have different dads. This is some pretty rich stuff, ladies, so let's get started—"

Choice scrolled her eyes over to Laqueeta and parked them there. She was thinking about her boys. They were classic examples of what Assistant Pastor Sensay was saying. She'd just spent the previous weekend with them; she should know.

****

All weekend, Laqueeta's boys had fought about everything—food, clothes, games, people, places and things. She could see that Mack, age 12, and the eldest by one year, thought he had it going-on over Mike. Mack was blessed to be growing into a wide receiver's body, while Mike was short and stubby like a little doughboy.

But that's not where their differences started or stopped. Although, neither of their dads was in the picture, Mack had gotten the idea that Laqueeta liked his dad best, and he felt it gave him one-up on his brother for their mother's affection. Both of the boys were beginning to experience the natural aggression that comes with puberty, but it was obviously compounded by the bitter competition for their mother's affection, which had been building between them throughout their childhood.

It was also clear that Laqueeta had never bothered to dispel the notion that she liked one of the dads over the other; especially, since the truth was, she loathed them both. But, more importantly, she hadn't had a heart-to-heart talk with her sons to let them know she loved them equally; and despite their differences, they were a family. Apparently, she had been too busy with her string of new boyfriends over the years while her son's lives were spinning out of control.

During one of their many fights that weekend, Mack let the secret slip that Laqueeta had entrusted with him.

"Mamma told me she was going to Vegas this weekend with her boyfriend; not you!" Mack twisted the knife into Mike's broken psyche. "She tells me plenty o' stuff she don't tell you. You ain't worth telling! Na-na-na-na!"

Choice's mind went ballistic. The only reason she'd agreed to keep the boys was that Laqueeta had begged her before one of their W.O.O.F. meetings.

****

"Hey, Choice." Laqueeta had smiled, gold tooth gleaming. "Just the person I want to see. I need to talk to you before the meeting."

"Okay." Choice breathed, bracing herself for some of Laqueeta's antics. "What's up?"

"Girl, I've got the chance of a lifetime!" Laqueeta fluffed her 'do. "My manager is gonna pay for me to take an all-expenses-paid, three-day trip to the Dental Assistants Conference in Pittsburg. This could make or break my career. And Girl, I'm so excited...except for one hitch."

Choice swallowed the bait. "What hitch?"

"What am I gonna do with my boys? They pretty big boys so I don't mind them coming home from school on they own, but I don't want 'em at the house all night by themselves. It's a crazy world out here."

"So, what do you want?" Choice pressed, tiring of the guessing game.

"I leave out on a Friday." Laqueeta explained. "Could my boys spend the night with you Friday night through Sunday? They got sleeping bags and everything. I'll be back Sunday night in plenty time to pick them up. What'cha say?"

"When is this trip?" Choice balked.

"Next week." Laqueeta snickered. "That should give you plenty time to get mentally prepared for my *bad* boys."

"And there's no other way?"

"Sis. Choice, I've thought and thought, and there's no one else I can turn to."

"Then, okay." Choice relented. "I'll do it for you…this time. They can stay at my place."

"That's so sweet of you." Laqueeta fluttered her spiky bought lashes. "It almost makes me wanna cry. I can't wait for the meeting to start so I can give my testimony. I'm gonna tell everybody just how sweet you are."

\*\*\*\*

And, now, to find out it had all been one giant hoax! Choice's mind raced off the charts when she recalled all she'd been through over the weekend with those heathen-acting boys, just so their mother could sneak off with some boyfriend. A boyfriend, she might add, which she had no business with in the first place. *What about her celibacy commitment to W.O.O.F.?*

Choice blasted Laqueeta with both barrels when she finally came slinking in to pick up the boys late Sunday night. "So how was your dental conference in Pittsburg?" Choice strained to control her rage. "The one that's gonna 'make or break your career'?"

"Oh, Girl, you know. I worked my little—"

"Save it!" Choice jumped in her face. "You left me here all weekend with your boys so you could shack-up with some man in Vegas? How dare you take advantage of me like that! We're supposed to be—"

"Now, hold on one minute, Miss Choice." Laqueeta backed to the door to escape her fury. "I didn't mean you no harm. I just didn't know what else to do—"

"I know what you could've done!" Choice blared. "You could've left me outta yo' mess; that's what you could've done! Instead, you're just a straight-up liar!"

"Uh-huh!" Laqueeta clenched her fists, readying for a major throw down. "Don't nobody talk to me like that in front of my boys!"

The boys were tipping downstairs, bags in hand. "Let's go, Mom," Mike whispered. "We're ready."

"You better be glad my boys are here, Choice King!" Laqueeta sprayed spit and strained against Mack as he pushed her toward the door. "I told you I didn't mean you no harm." She pointed a rainbow-tipped finger at her. "And that's as much as I'm gonna say 'bout it!"

"The last thing these boys, or any child, needs is a lying mamma!" Choice hurled. "I ought to tell Mother Brown and the others about your dirty, little secret—"

"You can tell 'em, smell 'em, go downtown and sell 'em for all I care!" Laqueeta lashed out as Mack and Mike pushed her through the door. "You think you're all-that, Choice King, but you ain't no better than me. You-you, cidity-acting-wannabe!"

"C'mon, Mom!" The boys pushed her toward the car.

"I'm sorry, Mack! I'm sorry, Mike!" Choice's voice trailed long after they were gone. She sank quietly to her knees. *Lord, please, don't let those poor boys end up...like me.*

****

"So, in conclusion, ladies," Assistant Pastor Sensay ended his talk, "I'm glad you've chosen abstinence before marriage, because the actions of parents can have a devastating impact on their children. Now, in the world's view, the statistics are stacked against single-parent households...low income; low parental involvement; low self-esteem. But here in the household of faith, all that can change. We *can* overcome the statistics."

The assistant pastor pin-pointed Rachael and Laqueeta with his stare. "You see, we are more than conquerors because Jesus forgives us and loves us, and you are not alone because W.O.O.F will walk beside you!" His vision widened. "And when we *truly* believe Jesus loves us, we'll be free to love others; otherwise, we'll always be too busy trying to fix ourselves. And if from here on out, we choose to do it God's way, everyone will benefit…our children, our families, our church, and our society at large."

Choice was so deep in thought, she didn't hear Sensay's closing remarks, nor did she hear him thank her for the invitation. Her eyes were locked on Laqueeta. *She's just like my so-called mom…a low-down, lying witch. All she ever thinks about is herself!*

"Choice! Choice!" Mother Brown rocked her shoulder after the meeting was over. "Are you okay?"

"Oh, I'm sorry." Choice came to herself as everyone was filing out of the meeting room, but she decided not to tell Mother Brown about Laqueeta's indiscretions in hopes she'd change. She would continue to pray for her, but mostly for her boys.

# CHAPTER 11: RECEIVE
## ONE ANOTHER.

*Romans 12:7*

With Mother Brown's help, Rachael and Jake moved into a pint-sized apartment on Thanksgiving eve, just over a year since her precious daughter, Lily's, death. "Don't worry about me; I'm blessed," is what Mother Brown said when she hugged Rachael and Jake goodbye. "The Lord's seen fit to give me six more daughters."

Rachael set up the one small bedroom for Jake, and she slept on the pull-out sofa that she'd managed to snag for a song from Goodwill. It was Saturday night, and she'd just tucked Jake in when her phone rang.

"Hi," the voice croaked. "It's me."

"Who?"

"Rachael, you've got to like help me!"

"Gabbi? Is this you?"

"Yes!" Gabbi squealed. "It's me."

"What's the matter?"

"I'm totally freaked." Gabbi sobbed. "I-I don't know what to do?"

"Gabbi, calm down and tell me what's wrong?" Rachael begged.

"I totally didn't know who else to call." Gabbi blubbered. "My parents are away in Europe for the season—"

"It's okay, Gabbi." Rachael tried to soothe her. "I'm glad you called; just tell me what's wrong."

"I kinda don't know how to tell you this." Gabbi sniffed. "But I know guys…lots of guys. The whole football team in fact."

"But, Gabbi, we—"

"Wait!" Gabbi's tears rolled backwards. "I never agreed to that celibacy and junk. That's you guys. I never joined the group; not really. I'm just Angel's ride; remember?"

"So, why're you so upset."

"After the game tonight, I was going to hook-up with the quarterback," she said in her preppy cheerleader voice, "but when I got to his room, Rach, there were three of them…him and two others."

"What?"

"Yes! They were all highed-up and stumbling drunk. The scene was way too intense for me!"

"So, what did you do?"

"I totally bolted!" Gabbi shrieked. "I got outta there…fast, but I can't stop thinking about what would've happened if I hadn't." Her tears started up again.

"So, where're you now?" Rachael asked.

"I don't know. I'm like totally lost. I mean I'm just driving around in circles somewhere, but that's why I called you. I didn't know who else to call."

"What about Angel?" Rachael pressed. "Where's Angel?"

"I don't know!" Gabbi screamed. "But I can't talk to her about this!"

"Why not? She's your roommate—"

"Don't you get it?" Gabbi yelled. "Angel only comes to church with you guys to play *Ms.-Goody-Two-Shoes* for her parents. She would totally do what I do if the guys would give her half a chance. But they think she's some kind of jock-lesbo or something 'cause she's tall and good at sports. But she would totally hook-up with any of these guys, if they'd have her."

"Angel?"

"Yes, Angel!" Gabbi screeched.

"Calm down, Gabbi."

"She totally thinks what I do is cool." Gabbi burst into a fresh stream of tears. "But it's not; it's not cool. I feel like all the guys are laughing at me behind my back, and all the girls; they just hate me. They hate me!"

"Gabbi-baby, you need to calm down. Where're you now?"

"I don't know. Somewhere near campus."

"Then head south." Rachael offered. "Come to Oak Cliff and see me."

"But—" Fear hung in Gabbi's voice. "You live with Mother Brown!"

"Not anymore," Rachael said proudly. "Me and Jake got our own place, now. Come on, Girl. You can sleep on my sofa and tell me all about it."

Gabbi sniffed. "You'd like do that for me?"

"Sure Gabbi." Rachael teased. "We're sisters, whether you like it or not."

"Oh, thanks. I like had nowhere else to turn. I called you 'cause I thought you'd understand about guys, since you have a baby and all—"

"To tell the truth, Gabbi, I've never been with any guy, except Tyrone…that one time…when my mamma wasn't home."

"Really? I'm just saying, you being from Oak Cliff and all, I thought—"

"Not so, Gabbi. But you come; spend the night; and we can go to church together tomorrow." Rachael chuckled uneasily. "Besides, it'll help me out, too."

"Why's that?"

"Tyrone wants to come over to see Jake and—"

"Mother Brown says you need a chaperone."

"I was going to have Tyrone meet us over at Mother Brown's, but now you can be my chaperone, Rachael said.

"Me? Chaperone?" Gabbi laughed so hard her shiny, new cell phone flipped shut.

****

That Sunday morning, Gabbi attended church with Rachael and Jake. This time, it was Rachael's turn to lend an outfit. The navel-naughty sweater and ultra-mini cheerleader skirt that Gabbi had shown up in at her apartment was a tad too inappropriate. She exchanged it for the plain black slacks and bulky hounds-tooth sweater that Rachael had found at a garage sale.

"This is so totally not me, Rachael," Gabbi said as she flipped her blonde hair over the sweater's edge. "But considering what would've happened, I'm like really, really grateful." She hugged Rachael and kissed Jake's soft, brown cheek. "I like totally thank you for being my sister."

Pastor Mayberry was in rare form that morning. He reigned over his beveled-edged crystal pulpit, back-lighted with a golden cross. He was draped from head to toe in a black pastoral robe, edged in African kente cloth. He was flanked on the left by Assistant Pastor Sensay Logan, handsomely sober in his white cleric collar and form-fitting black suit; and on his right, by none other than Evangelist Johnesther Mayberry, wearing a stunning ruby red wool suit with white-iced buttons and a flirty, red-laced hankie flattering the most jaw-dropping part of her anatomy. While enjoying her coveted position in the pulpit, she was careful to keep her curvaceous legs crossed at the ankles.

Pastor Mayberry brought a stirring message about the healing love of Jesus for the outcasts of the world. He centered his examples on New Testament women—the woman caught in the very act of adultery; the woman at the well with the five, would-be husbands; and the ex-prostitute who worshipped Jesus by anointing Him with the expensive ointment from her alabaster box.

After his rousing sermon, the Spirit was high and the choir was singing, "Come to Jesus." And by the time they reached the chorus, "He loves and forgives. He will break your chains and let you live," Gabbi's mind had flipped open, like her shiny, new cell phone. For the very first time, she saw the hold her sex addiction had on her life, and she wanted to be free, just like the women in Pastor Mayberry's sermon. Without any further prompting, Gabbi ran down the aisle, blue eyes streaming, blonde hair flapping.

Pastor Mayberry met her at the altar. "Daughter," he said, "no matter what you've done, Jesus loves you."

"But I'm like totally lost." Gabbi squealed. "I can't help myself. I can't find my way. I need Jesus!" In that moment, Gabbi trusted Christ to save her, and in her heart of hearts, she changed her mind and made a sincere commitment to W.O.O.F. She was well on the road to recovery.

During the entire scene, however, Angel was sitting primly at her parent's side. She was wearing a white, strait-laced collar under a black blazer. Her raven hair was pulled back into a tight bun. She'd joined the church some years before, but for the life of her she couldn't figure out what was happening now. In all her secret spaces, she would've traded places with Gabbi in a heartbeat. She longed for her popularity and the notoriety of being desired. She wanted desperately to take up with the boys—all the boys—where Gabbi had left off.

# CHAPTER 12: SUBMIT TO ONE ANOTHER.

*Ephesians 5:21*

Johnesther pounced on her husband as soon as they arrived home from church that Sunday. Her ruby red wool suit with the white-iced buttons was hitting all the right curves. "Mayberry!" She slammed her pearl and diamond earrings on the kitchen counter. "It's past time I became Co-Pastor of Overcoming Faith."

"Johnesther, what brought this on?"

"I'm an ordained minister, and when I'm Co-Pastor, I'll attract a slew of young women like that blonde who ran down the aisle this morning."

"As I understand it, Sis. Gabbi is already a member of W.O.O.F."

"W.O.O.F? Hmph! That doesn't matter. When I'm Co-Pastor, our church will attract all races, genders, creeds and kinds." Johnesther preached. "We'll put this city on notice that we believe in inclusion and equality, and our doors are open to everyone!" She swung back her shoulder-length hair. "And when I'm Co-Pastor, it'll set the right…image."

"Image?" Pastor Mayberry scowled. "People don't come to Christ based on image. They come to Him when they're drawn by the Spirit—"

"Mayberry, you're so old-school!" Johnesther sniped. "I can tell you don't know the first thing about modern church development. When I'm Co-Pastor, I'll have greater influence. I'll be more valuable—"

"Honey, that's not true. You have great value right now…as my wife, my helpmate, as a loving mother—"

"Don't talk to me about being a mother!" Johnesther snarled. "You don't know the first thing about being a mother!"

"Losing the baby hurt me too, honey," Pastor Mayberry said quietly. "But look at you…you've gone on to become a respected leader, a teacher, a minister of the Gospel…an evangelist for our Lord."

"That's not the same as being Co-Pastor—"

"And what about our Assistant Pastor—"

"Sensay? Who cares about Sensay?" Johnesther spouted. "He doesn't have a clue! He doesn't have the leadership skills to bring in the numbers like I can. All he's concerned about is that silly Children's Ministry—"

"Johnesther!"

"Don't Johnesther me! I know what I'm talking about. But it seems Sensay's gotten into your head. All you ever talk about is building that new Children's Education Building."

"It's important work, Johnesther. I thought you understood." Pastor Mayberry angled his head in disbelief. "You know if we can capture the minds and hearts of the young ones, maybe we won't have as many dysfunctional adults…drug addicts, violent predators, broken homes, broken families—"

"Honey, I'm not saying it's not important." The evangelist softened her tone. "I'm just saying when I'm Co-Pastor, it'll give me the power to bring in droves of new women. I could increase our numbers ten-fold! And with all the new women will come their children…and their money—"

"Tithes." Pastor Mayberry corrected.

Johnesther shook her hands to the heavens. "Don't you see, Mayberry? We can all prosper. Sensay can work with his precious children; the added funds will allow you to build the Children's Education Building that much faster; and I can address the unique needs women are facing today."

"And what about the men—"

"Men? Haven't you noticed, Mayberry, they're hardly any men left in the church—"

"And could that be because women are pushing men out of their rightful leadership roles?" Pastor Mayberry glared. "Besides, having a Co-Pastor is expressly against our church bylaws."

"Bylaws-Shmylaws! You know those bylaws aren't worth the paper they're written on. You can change those old things anytime you get ready—"

"That's not true, Johnesther." Pastor Mayberry sighed. "Our church bylaws represent the collective wisdom of our leadership and our congregation—"

"And you can fit all their wisdom on the head of a pin!"

"Be that as it may, our church doesn't believe two people can successfully hold one office." Pastor Mayberry explained.

"And why not?" Johnesther protested. "It's happening all over the land and country!"

"I know. And when it works, it's beautiful; but when it doesn't work—"

"But why wouldn't it work?"

"For the same reason Jesus said, 'No man can serve two masters.' He'll come to hate one and love the other. You know that."

"But we are one." Johnesther schmoozed. "We're husband and wife—"

"I know that; and they don't want a two-headed monster—"

"What?" Johnesther bristled.

"The church doesn't want marital issues between husband and wife to be drug into the pulpit and hurt the congregation."

"What marital issues? We don't have any marital issues!"

"Johnesther, you know very well the Bible says a husband wants *always* to please his wife." Pastor Mayberry moved in closer, but his wife shook off his intended embrace. He backed away and held onto the countertop and his temper. "And that being the case," he continued, "a congregation could very well suffer if the husband's desire to constantly please his Co-Pastor wife somehow overshadowed the needs and desires of the church as a whole. And what if the Co-Pastors had a difference of opinion?"

"That's stupid! And it would never happen with us." Johnesther blew. "Besides, that's beside the point—"

"No, Johnesther. That is the point. We serve at the behest of the leadership and the congregation. When I took on the role of Pastor, I agreed to be bound by the Bible and the church bylaws, which are based on biblical principles."

"Mayberry, I thought it was only those old fogies at the church that were keeping me from fulfilling my God-given destiny, but now I see it's you, too."

"Honey, sometimes you talk like nobody at church has the Holy Ghost but you." The pastor squinted. "So, could it be you've got the head knowledge, but not the heart to work with our people?"

Johnesther was on the verge of angry, hot tears. "Is it wrong for me to want our church to grow and be a force in this city, this world?"

"Johnesther, every church can't be a megachurch." The pastor reasoned. "The Lord adds souls as *He* sees fit."

"Mayberry, p-lease! Don't pretend you don't know there's an *art* to church growth. These megachurches don't just spring up overnight by chance; you know?"

"Of course, I know that Johnesther, but—"

"Look at me, Mayberry!" Johnesther traced her elegant form. "I'm not getting any younger, and I *need* to feel a sense of accomplishment before it's too late."

"Honey, I know the tragedy of losing our baby hurt you deeply—"

"Losing the baby?" Johnesther stared at him in disbelief. "Why on earth do you keep dredging up that ancient history?"

"Because bad things happen, but God is still a good God, and we can trust Him—"

"I know that!"

"Then why all this *hard-hearted* ambition?" Pastor Mayberry blared, straining to understand her point. "Where's it coming from?"

"Hard-hearted ambition? I don't have hard-hearted ambition!" Johnesther ranted. "I just want what's mine!"

"What?" The pastor threw up his hands. "I don't get it—"

"I just don't want to miss my due season…my breakthrough…my blessing!" His wife cried.

"Oh, Johnesther, don't you see?" Pastor Mayberry softened. "Everything the Lord's ever done for you is a blessing. And when the Lord gets ready for you to pastor, He'll make a way for that, too. You won't have to run over anything or anybody to get there. He'll—"

"So that's it, huh?" Johnesther said sourly. "You won't do this for me?"

"My darling wife, I can't—"

Johnesther flashed a *stop sign* to within an inch of her husband's nose and stormed upstairs before he could say another word.

Pastor Mayberry stayed behind in the kitchen to fry himself an egg for dinner.

# CHAPTER 13: LIE NOT TO ONE ANOTHER.

*Colossians 3:9*

"Well, Bliss, let's have it!" Evangelist Mayberry scolded over her cell phone as she sped up north to the Galleria Shops in her vintage two-seater Mercedes. It was Wednesday morning; the first big Red Apple sale before Christmas. "Come on, Bliss, I need to know. What happened at the Executive Board meeting last night?"

"Why're you asking me, *Sis. Legs*?" Deacon Bliss chided. "Didn't your husband tell you?"

"Bliss, stop it with the *Sis. Legs* nonsense!" Johnesther hissed. "And, no, he didn't tell me. We're not exactly on speaking terms just now." She failed to mention the pastor had pooh-poohed her latest co-pastor attempt.

"Oh?" Bliss drawled. "Trouble in paradise? Can I be of service?"

"Yes, you can." Johnesther fumed. "You can cut the crap and tell me what happened at the meeting."

"Temper-temper, First Lady." Bliss crooned. "It was a budget meeting. We discussed the budget."

"Did they review the bank statements?" Johnesther quizzed.

"Of course."

"And what did they say, particularly Mayberry?"

"Our illustrious Pastor was glad to see that the Annex *Fund* has grown from $2 million to nearly $3 million in just two quarters." Bliss feigned a pout. "But he was so disappointed that we're still a long way off from the construction goal of $6 million to build that Children's Education wing."

"Is that all he said about the Annex Fund?" Johnesther blistered.

"Well." Bliss toyed. "He did ask why the line item is labeled *Annex Fund,* instead of Children's Education Building Fund."

"And what did you say?" She snapped.

"I said what I was supposed to say. I told him *Annex Fund* was just a shorter name. Besides, we don't want to confuse it with our General Building Fund; now do we?" Bliss chuckled.

"Did he fall for that?" Johnesther drilled.

"Of course, he did. I'm the Finance Director."

"But did he figure out—"

"Of course not."

"So, he still doesn't know only we can get our hands on that money in the Annex Fund?" Johnesther pressed.

"Nope." Bliss snorted. "Since the rest of the accounts require me, Sensay, and the Pastor to sign, they quite naturally assume all the accounts are set up that way."

"So, the $3 million is totally under our control?"

"Well, of course! What've I been saying? Haven't you been listening?" The deacon growled. "Only *our* names…mine and yours…are on the signature card for the Annex Fund. And only *I* have access to all the signature cards. It's a lock."

"Did they ask about the General Building Fund?"

"Yep, they asked about it, and I told them the truth. The General Building Fund is just for repairs and things around the church. Since the Fellowship Hall is fairly new, and we just put a new roof on the sanctuary last year, I convinced them the General Building Fund should be kept at a minimum, somewhere under $20,000."

"And the General Building Fund account—"

"Don't get greedy, Johnesther. It requires me, Pastor and Sensay to sign, just like all the rest," Bliss said plainly. "But make no mistake; the lion's share of the church's money is going into our Annex Fund."

"So, with the Annex Fund nearing $3 million, it's time to move forward with our plans for the satellite church instead of that silly-ole Children's Education wing." Johnesther firmed.

"Yep, it's ripe for the pickin'." Bliss smiled. "And I can see it all now…we'd have Overcoming Faith-Southside and Overcoming Faith-Northside—"

"And I'll be the pastor on the Northside where people have vision…and money." Johnesther's voice warmed. "Mayberry doesn't get it yet, but it'll be grand. In just a few months, we'll raise enough money on the Northside to pay back the Annex Fund and build that Children's Education Building…for cash—"

"And then he'll understand." Deacon Bliss surmised.

"Who knows? Mayberry may never understand, but I bet the rest of that money-hungry Southside crowd will, and they'll praise me for my vision."

"I'm still easing the satellite church idea in on the Trustees and Deacons," Bliss buzzed. "I'm telling 'em a satellite church will bring in extra tithes and help us build that prized Children's wing that much faster."

"Be careful." Johnesther cautioned. "We don't want Mayberry to find out."

"I know. I'm just spoon feeding 'em, and I didn't' let on you had nothing to do with it."

"How's it going?"

"They're a little slow to catch on, but sooner or later we'll need them to vote to use the Annex Fund for the satellite church instead of the Children's wing." Bliss crowed.

"I'm still working the hat-wearing senior women, too; even those ole plain-Jane biddies that hang around Mother Brown." Johnesther brightened. "And with a little work, I've got a feeling they'll all come around to our way of thinking."

"We've got the plan—"

"We've got the money." Johnesther giggled. "We can't go wrong! See you, Bliss. I'm gonna shop 'til I drop!"

\*\*\*\*

Later that day, before the W.O.O.F meeting, Choice tapped on Assistant Pastor Sensay's office door and stuck her head in. "Hope I'm not disturbing you," she said gently.

Sensay dropped his pen and stood at attention. Her rich melodic voice had that effect on him. "No, Sis. Choice," he stammered. "Come on in."

"You remember my name?" Choice smiled from under her lavish lashes. "I'm impressed."

"Who could forget?" Sensay said self-consciously. "Please. Have a seat."

"I won't keep you." Choice eased into the chair. "I really came to apologize."

"Apologize? For what?"

"I got so wrapped up in your message that night I forgot to present this to you." Choice held up the silver gift bag stuffed with gold paper. "I've been meaning to bring it by. It's from all of us in W.O.O.F. We really want to thank you. We've started to see family...and our relationship to it...in a totally new way."

"You're most welcome." Sensay smiled and the room brightened. "But I have to admit, I'm not usually around that many women at once."

"Oh, no?" Choice chuckled. "I would've taken you for quite the ladies' man."

"You're kidding; right?" Sensay flushed. "I don't know the last time I've been alone in the company of a lady."

"Oh?"

"Present company excluded, of course." He squirmed.

"Well, I'll go now. W.O.O.F. meeting will be starting soon." Choice rose to leave. "We hope you enjoy the gift."

Sensay touched the graceful hand that was planted on his desktop. He could feel the heat rising in his chest. "Don't go," he said. "Please. I've wanted to talk to you."

"About what?" Choice tensed.

"About me...and you," Sensay said. "What would I have to do to get to know you better?"

"Me? Why would you want to get to know somebody like me?" Choice scrambled for the door, and he met her there.

"Because I think you're a fascinating woman," Sensay said flatly, "and I won't be satisfied until you prove me wrong."

Choice looked puzzled. "I'm sure I'll get that by the time I get home."

"See." Sensay smiled. "It's the things you say...your simplicity...your complexity. You're like a cross between...white slacks and collard greens, and it makes me want to know the woman inside."

"I don't think that's possible. I'd better go—"

Choice attempted an escape, but Sensay held onto her hands. "Just have coffee with me, or lunch." He offered. "You decide."

"W.O.O.F women don't date without a chaperone."
Choice stiffened.

"It's not a date…just coffee. I promise. You'll be safe
with me."

"I don't know—"

"Just a minute." Sensay pulled out his cell phone and
hit speed dial. "Hello. Yes, ma'am. Would it be okay with
you if I took Choice out to coffee or lunch? Yes, ma'am,
it'll be in the daytime. Yes, ma'am, she can just meet me
at the restaurant. No, ma'am, I promise I won't follow her
home. Thank you, Mother Brown."

"Assistant Pastor!"

"Your chaperone says it's okay." Sensay smiled,
pleased to have out-maneuvered her defenses. "Now,
what do you say?"

Choice was laughing so hard she could barely answer.
"Well, Assistant Pastor Sensay Logan, if you'd go all out
for me like that and haggle with Mother Brown, I guess I
can only say, yes."

"From now on, it's just Sensay; okay? I'll call you later,
and we can set the time."

"Well, okay, you crazy person." Choice smiled on her
way out. "Okay-then."

# CHAPTER 14: HAVE COMPASSION FOR ONE ANOTHER.

*I Peter 3:8*

On Friday, just before the clock struck noon, Evangelist Mayberry paid a surprise visit to Bliss Enterprises at the nearby Redbird Airport Industrial Park. His secretary had already gone to lunch when Johnesther arrived, so she strolled into Bliss' corporate office without knocking.

"And to what do I owe this pleasure?" Deacon Bliss glanced up from his lavish granite desk, never breaking the crease in his heavily starched smile.

"Cut the crap, Bliss," Evangelist Mayberry rebutted. "I'm here to talk about our next move…and that's all."

"But it could be oh-so much more." Bliss gave her a sexy wink.

Johnesther ignored his incessant flirting and took a seat in front of his desk. "I can't very well camp out in your office at the church. Tongues would wag," she said. "So, I came to you, and I must say, you've got a very impressive operation."

"You bet." Bliss hoisted his chest. "It gives me the time and the money to do what we want to do at the church."

"And that's why I'm here." Johnesther crossed her legs to get a rise out of him. Her ankle boots with the gold chains were very flattering to her voluptuous calves. "What're you hearing from the leadership about the satellite church idea?"

"I've been hitting up the old boys as hard as I can without getting their dander up." Bliss admitted.

"And what're they saying?"

"I've been hinting that it's time for us to expand to Overcoming Faith-Northside."

"And—" Evangelist Mayberry braced herself.

"And I think they'll go for it, but first we've got to get the membership numbers up at Overcoming Faith-Southside."

"But why does that matter?" Johnesther pouted.

"They'd just feel better branching out to the Northside if it looks like we're outgrowing ourselves down here on the Southside."

"Whatever!" Johnesther uncrossed her legs and re-crossed them at the ankles.

"The more warm bodies filling the seats, the easier it'll be to make our move." Bliss urged.

"To tell the truth, I'm getting some hesitation from the senior women, too." Johnesther flustered. "But I'm starting to get the sense they'll vote to use the Annex Fund for a satellite church—"

"Instead of the Children's Education Building?"

"Yes, if we can convince them it would mean more outreach in North Dallas," Johnesther said. "Even the senior women realize the day of the Black church and the

White church is dead and gone. This is the Age of Inclusion. It's time for all races to worship together."

"Well, if that's all they need, I'm sure we can trot out some good outreach statistics to get 'em chompin' at the bits." Bliss encouraged.

"Of course, we can. We'll come up with something."

"Then what about the young folk? Won't they be more likely to vote for a Children's Education Building?"

"These young people don't vote!" Johnesther blared. "The few young men we've got are too busy running behind their *boyfriends*." She smirked. "And the young women are too busy dropping babies by who knows who to come to a church business meeting and vote."

"True-dat." Bliss laughed. "Only the old-heads will vote."

"So aside from the Deacons and Trustees, we only need to get the widows and married women voting our way."

"But what about—"

"The married men?" Johnesther preened. "They're so hen-pecked; they'll do whatever their wives say."

"Johnesther, you're scandalous! Just scandalous!"

"You just keep after the men, and I'll keep working the women."

Bliss rubbed his hands together. "If we can figure out a way to drive up the membership numbers, I believe we'll have enough votes to use the Annex Fund for the satellite church—"

"And squash that silly, little Children's Education Building…at least for now."

"You got it, Baby!"

"Got to go." Johnesther sashayed to the door in a hip-hugging suede skirt that swished above her calves. She stopped at the door, looked back over her shoulder and flashed her lashes. "Don't worry, Bliss. Between the two of us, we'll find a way to drive up those membership numbers…in spite of the likes of Mayberry and Sensay."

****

Meanwhile, Sensay and Choice had agreed to meet for lunch on the other side of the airport. A new coffee chain had chanced to move in on the Southside, across from Redbird Mall. They both decided it would be a good idea to support it, at least while it lasted.

"Waiting long?" Choice tapped Sensay's shoulder when she arrived.

"Not long." Sensay smiled up at her. Choice smiled back, and all seemed right in his world. She stripped off her navy pee-jacket to a simple pair of straight-leg jeans and a red turtleneck, but to Sensay she looked like a reigning princess.

Choice slid across from him in the booth, laying her jacket and purse to one side. "Okay, this is your party." She smirked. "What do you want from me?"

"Just to talk."

"Then talk," Choice said in a tone intended to push him away.

Sensay didn't bite. "Lunch first," he said and went to the counter to order for them. He brought back two trays.

"This looks good." Choice admired her tuna salad sandwich.

"Sure does," Sensay said, enchanted by the curve of her luscious lips.

"It pays to come to new places while they're still trying to make a good impression," Choice remarked.

"See, that's why I like you." Sensay chuckled. "You know how to size a thing up and call it like you see it."

"And that's a good quality?" Choice widened her eyes. "I thought it just got on everybody's nerves."

"So how did you get so wise?" Sensay volleyed.

"Surely, you jest." Choice flicked the ball back into his court.

"Come on, Choice." Sensay entreated. "Tell me a little about yourself."

"Do you really want to know?" Her eyes flashed him a *fasten-your-seatbelt* warning. "Are you sure?"

"I do."

"Okay, here it goes." Choice leaned back in the booth and cast her eyes toward the red-lighted exit sign. "I grew up in Nashville. I couldn't wait to get out of there, so I ran away from home as soon as I graduated high school. I haven't been back since."

"Why not?"

"Nothing to go back to."

"Do you keep up with your folks?"

"I used to."

"So how did you get to Dallas?"

"Don't know." Choice took a big bite of her sandwich.

"You don't know?"

Choice raised her hands. "You ask me to tell you the truth, and when I do you can't handle it."

"But how can you not know how you got here?" Sensay pressed.

"I was high; okay." Choice tilted back her head to stave off the tears. "I was too ramped-up on coke, and speed, and who-knows-what to know how I got here, or with whom."

"Choice—"

"Choice, what? That's just how it was back then, Rev."

"I kinda knew you were no church-girl, but—"

"You wanted to know how I got so *worldly* wise; didn't you?" Choice knifed. "I got that way on the streets of downtown Dallas, dodging cops, panhandling for drugs, squatting in shelters—"

"Were you a prostitute?" Sensay cringed.

"Nope," Choice said flatly. "I overdosed before it came to that. But make no mistake, that's where I was headed...for sure."

"Choice, I never would've guessed. You have such...serenity. Nothing about you says...street."

"I had a decent upbringing, I guess." Choice shrugged. "We just had…issues; that's all."

"And how did you get to Overcoming Faith?"

"The long way 'round."

"Explain."

"Twelve Steps. Rehab. Walking away from my past.

"Oh, I see."

"But church folk can be some hard folk to deal with, Sensay. Sometimes, they make you feel like running back to where you came from—"

"Choice—"

"Don't worry; I won't." Choice squeezed back a tear. "I can't."

"Why not?"

"For me, it was Jesus or die." Choice confided. "And I chose Jesus."

"Tell me more." Sensay's pulse quickened. "I just love hearing how our Lord restores—"

"That's 'cause you're a restorer of sorts yourself." Choice polished off her sandwich in one big gulp. "Your turn."

"Well, I grew up right here in Oak Cliff; all the right schools…Turner, Atwell, and Carter High."

"Local boy makes good, huh?"

"Graduated Denton College and went on to seminary at Dallas—"

Just then Choice's cell phone rang, and she flipped it open. "Excuse me, Sensay. I need to take this."

"No prob—"

"She what? You what? You want me to what? Are you kidding me? No way! Forget it! I have a church home…Overcoming Faith!" Choice snapped her cell phone shut.

Sensay watched as confusion clouded her eyes. "What's the matter?"

"Nothing." Choice grabbed her purse. "Gotta go."

"You're obviously too upset to drive." Sensay caressed her hand. "Take a minute. Breathe. Tell me what's wrong; maybe I can help."

"You can't help me." Choice's body sank. "Nobody can help me."

"What happened?"

Choice's mouth curled into an odd smile. "Death…in the family."

"Who?"

"My mom…my aunt—"

"Which one?"

"Both…neither." Choice staved off the tears. "It's a long story."

"So, when's the funeral?"

"Don't know." Choice's bottom lip tightened. "Can't go."

"But Choice—"

"Won't go!" She grabbed up her things and ran out.

\*\*\*\*

Later on that same Friday night, Tyrone Paige rang Mother Brown's doorbell. He was starting to get the hang of these chaperoned visits. In fact, he rather enjoyed them. Although he was glad Rachael and Jake finally had their own place, coming to Mother Brown's felt like family. Tyrone was bracing against the cold with his hands jammed into a gray fleece hoodie when she answered the door.

"Take off that silly cap and come in out of the cold," Mother Brown greeted. "I just don't understand why y'all have to wear those things with the tag still hanging on it."

"Because—"

"Never mind." Mother Brown stopped him. "I'm sure I won't understand it any better than why you wear your pants sagging." She smiled playfully. "Anyhow, take a seat. Rachael and Jake are in the kitchen."

"Kitchen?" Tyrone quipped. "I didn't know Rachael knew her way into a kitchen."

"Don't be smart." Mother Brown eyed him into a seat. "We all have to find our way sooner or later."

"Yes, ma'am," Tyrone said, and rounded the dining room table to kiss Iris on her cheek. She gave him a toothy grin, holding court from her booster chair, fork in hand.

"Don't worry, Mother Brown." Tyrone smiled. "I took your advice."

"What advice?"

"I got a job," Tyrone said. "I got my own place—"

"You did? But how? What about your parents?"

"They didn't like it at first, but I had to do it."

"But why now?" Mother Brown puzzled.

"My mom never liked Rachael." Tyrone shook his head. "I don't know why. It wasn't Rachael's fault she got pregnant; it was mine. But because of the bad blood, Rachael won't let Jake go over there, so I had to go."

"And—"

"And…I'm working and finishing up my mechanics course…part time."

"That's good, Tyrone." Mother Brown's eyes lit up her lenses. "I'm proud of you, and I'm sure Rachael will be, too."

"I'm not quite ready to tell Rach; not just yet," Tyrone stammered.

"But why?"

"She'll get all excited, and I'm not where I want to be yet. I had to move in with my cousin. We've got roommates—"

"Well, it's your story to tell, Tyrone, and when you tell it is up to you." Mother Brown lodged her tongue firmly in her cheek. "But I see you didn't accept my invitation."

"What?"

"About coming to church."

"Oh, I'm gonna have to work up to that one, too." Tyrone shrugged. "But I can see it's been real good for Rach and Jake."

"You can see that; can you?"

"Rachael seems a lot more at ease lately, and besides growing like a weed, Jake's just downright happy." Tyrone grinned.

"Every child needs a consistent place and consistent people to feel safe, Tyrone." Mother Brown smiled. "And Rachael is like a daughter to me. We're building a family at Overcoming Faith."

"Here it comes!" Rachael announced. Jake brought in a bowl of mashed potatoes, taking special care not to spill it. Rachael followed with a bowl of fresh green beans smothered in smoked turkey, and a basket of hot rolls. "Be right back." Rachael sat it down gently and rushed back to the kitchen. She returned with a steaming platter of baked chicken and gravy.

"Wow!" Tyrone's eyes stretched. "You did all this?"

"Yes." Rachael smiled. Her ponytail had given way to a sleek hairdo that fell to her shoulders, and she was wearing a pretty red cardigan with winter white slacks. Her eyes were shining like new money, too; delighted to have her whole family under one roof. "I made it all from scratch, and Mother Brown helped."

"Yeah," Jake chimed in. "Mother Brown's a...a genius."

Iris squealed her agreement.

"She sure is." Tyrone helped Jake into his seat at the table. Then he reached around him to hold Rachael's hand. "Thank you for going to all the trouble."

"No trouble at all." Rachael squeezed Tyrone's hand in return. "Actually, it was fun."

"Let us pray," Mother Brown said, and they all bowed their heads like it was Christmas dinner, just a few weeks early.

# CHAPTER 15: FELLOWSHIP WITH ONE ANOTHER.

*I John 1:7*

The week after the ball dropped in Time's Square to usher in the New Year, 2008 was well underway. The Overcoming Faith Executive Board met on Wednesday afternoon to review their annual plans. Deacon Bliss was beside himself throughout the meeting. He could hardly wait until it concluded to call Evangelist Mayberry.

"Did I catch you at a bad time?" Bliss buzzed over his church phone.

"Bliss?" Johnesther thrashed around in her flannel robe and house shoes. "Why're you calling me at home?"

"Yo' cell phone is turned off, or something. I couldn't reach you." Deacon Bliss muffled his voice. "But I need to talk to you before Pastor gets home from the Board meeting."

"Why?" Johnesther whispered, following his lead. "What happened?"

"It nearly turned into a mess, but I held down the fort." Bliss bragged.

"What? What?"

"Pastor saw the Annex Fund had grown to over $3 million, and he got a briar under his saddle to go ahead and build that dang Children's Education Building."

"But how?" Johnesther quivered. "I thought it would cost $6 million to build?"

"It will…that or more. But Pastor said since the fund is growing at such a fast clip, we oughta just borrow against it and go ahead and get started—"

"Oh, no!" Johnesther yelped.

"But I said, 'In this down economy, it's better to wait and build up our war chest before we build.'" Bliss crowed.

"Good!"

"Yeah, but Pastor said, 'Every day we wait the price of building materials is going up. We don't want to lose ground by waiting too long.'"

"And what did you say?" Johnesther squeezed.

"I said, 'But we don't want to put the church at risk by drowning it in a bunch o' debt.' And then I said, 'The only way to build faster is to get more tithe-paying members.'"

"And what did my illustrious husband have to say to that?"

"He was left with his mouth hanging like a Bo-Bo." Bliss chortled. "And I said, 'Pastor, have you ever considered having a satellite church in North Dallas? That could do the trick—'"

"What happened then?"

"The Deacons and Trustees got real quiet 'cause they didn't wanna let on to Pastor they'd already been discussing it amongst themselves." Bliss chuckled with pride. "And that's how I saved the day and put the skids to the notion of going into debt to build that sissy Children's wing.

"Good boy!" The knot in Johnesther's stomach relaxed. "So how did you leave it?"

"I told them if we can get the membership numbers up, somehow, the Annex Fund would grow that much faster."

"Yes." Johnesther agreed. "And that fit right in with what you'd been telling the men all along."

"Sure did. They were drooling at the mouth by the time I got through—"

"But what did Mayberry say?"

"He couldn't say much." Bliss snickered. "By that time, they were pressuring Pastor to come up with ways to increase our numbers. And they said, 'For *whatever* it is we decide to do with the Annex Fund.'"

"*Whatever?*" Johnesther salivated. "So, they left the door wide open for us to use the Annex Fund for my satellite church...and trash that Children's Education Building?"

"You got it, Pretty Lady! They didn't say it outright, but I've been pumping the swing votes on the Deacon Board, and they'll see it our way if we can get our membership numbers up."

"And Mayberry still hasn't figured out the Annex Fund is in our names only?"

"Nope. Bless his soul; he's still in the dark as always." Bliss hooted.

Johnesther chuckled. "Good."

"Right as rain, Suga…right as rain! Only the two of us…together…can sign for that $3-plus-million."

"Only the two of us…together." Johnesther threw her favorite wolf a morsel. "I must admit, Bliss, it does have a nice ring."

Bliss lapped it up, tail wagging. "That's what I've been trying to tell you, Sis. Legs. I'm the man you need." He grinned. "We'll either get the votes to scrap the Children's wing and use the Annex Fund for the satellite church—"

"Or we'll take the Annex Fund and start our own church." Johnesther rustled. "Either way, I'll get to pastor my church up in North Dallas!"

"Now, don't let on to the Pastor," Bliss buzzed. "I just wanted you to know this before he got home."

"I'm glad you called," Johnesther said, peeling off her robe and house shoes. She quickly traded them for a black negligee and silk slippers. "I hadn't planned to look cute or fix dinner tonight, but now I will. I'll cook Mayberry all his favorites and soften him up for our next move."

"So, have you come up with a way to grow the flock so the satellite idea can fly?" Bliss queried.

"Not just yet, but now that I know the deacons are behind us, I'll pray about it." The evangelist added.

"Pray about it?" Bliss snarled. "You've got to make another run at the Pastor, and this time, make it stick."

"You can bet on it!" Johnesther admired herself in the mirror. "Thank you, Bliss. Got to go rattle some pots and pans."

****

"Well, hello, Miss Rachael." Deacon Bliss' receptionist curled her lips in displeasure. "Why am I not surprised to see you?"

"I just came by to drop off our monthly report," Rachael quickly explained. "Actually, I'm on my way to the W.O.O.F. meeting."

"Uh-huh." The receptionist rolled her eyes. "Anyway, Deacon Bliss said to send you in *whenever* you stop by." She flashed her thumb toward his door. "Go. He's in there."

Rachael tapped lightly and leaned in. "Uhh...excuse me."

"Well...come in," the deacon crooned, as he was hanging up on his call with Johnesther. "Now, ain't this an unexpected pleasure."

"I hope I'm not disturbing you, Deacon Bliss—"

"How many times do I have to tell you to call me Ray?" He jumped up to clear a seat for her. "Sit down, Rachael. Sit down."

"Well, Deacon Ray, I brought by the monthly report, but I need to talk to you, too."

"You can talk to me any time—"

"W.O.O.F. has been thinking about starting an Investment Club."

"Oh?"

"Yes, we've discussed it with Mother Brown, and she thinks it's a good idea, too."

"Why on earth do y'all need an Investment Club?"

"We want to be independent. We don't want money to affect...our decisions."

"I don't get it." Bliss curled his thick lips. "Your decisions about what?"

"Our decisions about dating...or anything else."

"Oh, you mean y'all don't wanna have to give it up to no man to get yo' bills paid." The deacon laughed.

"It's not funny to us." Rachael flared. "Mother Brown says we need a strategy, and this Investment Club will give us access to funds without having to ask anyone outside of W.O.O.F."

"So y'all plan to make loans and such?" Bliss inquired.

"Yes. We'll each put in a certain amount every month, based on our income. And should we need a short-term loan for some emergency, we'll be able to get what we've put in," Rachael explained.

"But what if you need more than what you've put in?"

"We'll ask W.O.O.F for permission to borrow more and set up a payment plan, with no interest."

"I'd have to see the idea on paper first." Bliss shrugged.

"But it can work, Deacon Ray. We know it can."

"So, you really want this, huh, Rachael?" Bliss undressed her with his eyes.

"Of course, I do," she said self-consciously. "We all do."

"Then just for you, Suga, I'll see what I can do." Bliss came around his desk and brushed his hand gently across her cheek. "In fact, I'd do just about anything to make you happy."

Rachael flinched and backed into her chair. "Deacon Bliss!"

"I see you can't take the hints I've been throwing yo' way, so I'll come right out with it." The desire thickened in his voice. "I want to take care of you, Rachael…and little man."

Rachael gripped her locket like it was a shield. "But you're married," she said.

"That may be true, for now." Bliss pulled his chair around to box her in, knees-to-knees. "But it doesn't have to stay true, forever. If we can find a way to get along, that can be fixed."

Rachael squeezed her locket. "What're you saying?"

"I'm saying I want you to be my woman…have my son—"

"I can't—"

"With just the right humph," the deacon said, sliding his knees between hers, "who knows what can happen?"

"Quit that!" Rachael pushed past him and escaped. "That'll never happen!"

Bliss beat her to the door and blocked her exit. "Never say never." He moaned, desire steaming from his nostrils. "You need things. Little man needs things. And I can give you all that and more when you're mine."

"Why do you keep messing with me?" Rachael fumbled behind him to reach the knob.

"You're a disturbing woman, Rachael Jones." Bliss breathed in her cologne. "Every time I see you, you turn me on; and I haven't had a woman turn me on in a long, long time."

"Just stop it!" Rachael stood back in her legs and clamped her arms tight across her chest. "If you don't let me out of here this instant, I'm gonna scream my head off!"

Bliss stepped aside, but he caught her trembling hand as she reached for the knob. "I can do things for you no other man can do." He sweated in her ear. "I just want you to think about that."

Rachael snatched open the door. "You can set up our Investment Club; that's what you can do!" She slammed the door behind her, equally disturbed and relieved that his receptionist had left for the day.

"Rachael Jones!" Fancy fastened onto her elbow as she scurried into the hallway. "Every time I see you, you're up in Deacon Bliss' face. What's up with that?"

"Fancy?" Rachael shook loose her arm. "What're you talking about?"

"You don't know, huh? So, where're you coming from now?"

Rachael shrugged her shoulders. "Have you forgotten? I'm the secretary/treasurer of W.O.O.F. It's my job to drop off our monthly report and discuss our Investment Club."

"Don't think you can make points with Deacon Bliss." Fancy bristled. "He's a married man, and he's far too important for the likes of you—"

"Just quit it, Fancy!" Rachael's nerves drummed against her temples. "I don't know what your problem is, Girl, but you'd better back up off o' me."

"I don't have a problem!" Fancy seethed. "I just know your kind. Women like you are always trying to worm in where you don't belong." She gave her eyes the two-finger stab and pointed them back at Rachael. "But I've got my eyes on you."

Rachael drew in a long, deep breath. "Fancy, what is it with you? Every time we try to reach out to you…you start acting the fool."

"Hasn't anybody told you, Rachael Jones?" Fancy added a hand to the dip of her narrow hips. "This is a dog-eat-dog world, and it's every dog for herself. I joined W.O.O.F. for my own reasons. I don't need you…any of you!"

Rachael's face flared from hot to hotter. She wanted to take Fancy right then and there; snatch off that high-dollar weave and stuff it down her evil throat. But then she remembered; she was at church. Ears smoking, she twirled on her heels and sped off to the meeting room.

At the other end of the hall, Choice was entering the church from the back parking lot. Who did she see but Laqueeta, sneaking out of some man's car on her way to the W.O.O.F meeting? Choice was blazing, but she pretended not to see her plant a kiss on the man so strong it could grow hair. *What should I expect from the likes of her? She's no better than my own lying mom. Hypocrite! I'm glad she died and took all her lies to the grave with her.*

Choice beat Laqueeta into the meeting room so she wouldn't have to look at her. *I ought to tell Mother Brown, but it wouldn't do any good; not even she can help Laqueeta. She's a lost cause! I'll just keep praying for her poor, mixed-up boys.*

# CHAPTER 16: USE HOSPITALITY
## ONE TO ANOTHER.

*I Peter 4:9*

This time it was Fancy's turn to invite Evangelist Mayberry to lunch. Among other things, it would give her a chance to wear her new knitted mink jacket to the Renaissance Hotel. The Christmas purchase had taken the last of her credit cards over the limit, but who cared? It was a new year, and it was to be her big year! By the end of June, she'd pass the bar; and by the fall, she'd be the managing attorney for a growing Overcoming Faith Church.

While the rest of the world was ringing in the New Year, however, Fancy hadn't heard a peep out of Johnesther throughout the holidays; not even so much as a greeting card. But with the juicy gossip she had to offer, now, Fancy was sure she'd win back her undivided attention and lock-in her lucrative career plans. In fact, the news she was packing was so rich, Fancy fully expected Johnesther would pick up the tab.

They met at their usual table, which was hard to come by on a Saturday afternoon; but Fancy's well-placed bribe had done the trick.

"I was surprised by your call." Johnesther glimmered in her silver-fox trimmed suit and silver-gray stilettos. She'd come dripping in diamonds for the expressed purpose of getting a rise out of Fancy. She wanted to rub her jealous streak raw, just for the fun of it.

"I'm so glad you found the time to join me," Fancy said, with a shaky smile.

By the time their waiter came and went, Johnesther wanted to get down to it. "So why did you ask me to meet you here today, Fancy, pray tell?"

"I wanted to…share a few tidbits I've gathered here and there." Fancy smirked. "You know, the kind of thing any good lawyer does for her client."

"And I'm sure you'll be one of the best, if you pass the bar—"

"When I pass the bar," Fancy's voice spiked, "I'll be ready to represent Overcoming Faith in all of its business matters by the fall."

Johnesther pursed her lips. *Oh, my, here we go again! This little girl doesn't know who she's messing with.*

Failing to register Johnesther's lack of interest, Fancy's words spewed like a busted faucet. "I've piled up my hours. I've worked two jobs…overtime." Her hands began to tremble. "I've purposely trained to handle all facets of church business. Non-profit law is my specialty…churches, charities, foundations—"

"Oh, I see," Johnesther said to cut off her water, and she finally noticed the dark circles under Fancy's eyes and her ratty-tat braids, which were totally uncharacteristic. "Sounds pretty intense." Johnesther smirked. "You must be exhausted."

"Exhausted?" Fancy sagged. "Oh, yes...I am...*really*...tired—"

"So then tell me, my dear." Johnesther jiggled her knobs to shut off the drip. "Why'd you bring *me* here?"

"Oh, I'm sorry, Evangelist." Fancy re-focused her scrambled brain. "Do you know Rachael Jones?"

"Rachael Jones...of W.O.O.F. fame?"

"Yes, the very same." Fancy confirmed. "She and her kid were virtually homeless until Mother Brown took them in and helped Rachael get on her feet."

"Oh, really?"

"Can't you see she dresses out of the thrift store?"

"I hadn't noticed." Johnesther forked the food around on her plate.

"Well, take my word for it; homeless women like Rachael are always trying to get next to people with money—"

"How well I know," Johnesther said flatly, trying not to let on she'd done some digging into Fancy's background, as well.

"But did you know she's been trying to get next to Deacon Bliss—"

"Bliss!" Johnesther's fork hit the floor.

"Yes, I caught Rachael coming out of his office...alone...and she got real nervous when she saw me."

"We can't have that!" Johnesther flushed. "Bliss is a married man, and it would be an embarrassment to our church if she forced herself on him."

"That's why I thought you should know."

"Besides, Deacon Bliss and I collaborate on budget matters from time to time...to help the Pastor, of course. We can't very well continue that practice if he's somehow involved with a single woman at the church."

"Don't worry." Fancy pursed her trembling lips. "It won't get far. I've got my eye on that girl."

"Then, do, dear; keep me posted." The evangelist granted her a half-smile.

"But that's not all." Fancy pressed.

"No?"

Fancy dropped to a low whisper. "Did you know Assistant Pastor Sensay Logan is having an affair with a W.O.O.F. member, too?"

"No! Who?" Johnesther flapped.

Fancy pulled back, ever mindful of her ambitions. "Is this information of value to you, Evangelist?"

Johnesther squeezed her for the last drop. "It is valuable, my dear...unless it's tainted with greed."

Fancy gripped her temples. "Do you see my dream to be the church's lead attorney as greed?"

"Not in the least." Johnesther allowed her some slack. "I only find your attempt to leverage your ambitions at this moment, very ill-timed."

"But I'm not—"

"So, with whom is Sensay having an affair?"

"Choice King."

"That tall, wooly-headed girl?" Johnesther frowned.

"Yes. I spotted them coming out of a coffee shop in the Redbird area. They were alone, together, when everybody knows W.O.O.F. members have taken a vow not to date, un-chaperoned." Fancy failed to mention it was not a vow, but a strategy; and it was broad open daylight.

"How unsavory." Johnesther curled up her nose. "The man can't expect to have a successful career at our church by sneaking around with unattached females."

"Here, again, Evangelist, I see it as my duty to protect the church's interests." Fancy dribbled. "I'm only confiding this information—"

"Just keep me posted." Johnesther motioned for their waiter. "Check, please!"

# CHAPTER 17: FOREBEAR ONE ANOTHER.

*Ephesians 4:2*

Meanwhile, across town on the Southside that Saturday afternoon, Choice was on a cleaning binge in her small townhouse apartment. Reluctantly, she answered the knock at her door.

"Oh, no!" Choice shrilled. "How'd you find me?" She attempted to slam the door in the woman's face.

"Don't, Choice!" The woman braced her sizable weight against the door. "I found your address through your church. We need to talk."

Choice thought for a moment before attempting to slam the door in her face again. "Just go away! I've got nothing to say to you!"

"Please, Choice." The woman hung onto the knob. "No matter how you feel, we're family. I just want to talk, and when I've said my piece, I'll leave you alone—"

"Promise?"

"Yes, I promise." The woman relented. "I'm tired, too."

Slowly, Choice eased open the door. "All right, come in, Mom...Aunt," she taunted, "or should I just call you...Liar?"

"I know how you must feel, Choice." Marian King collapsed onto the sofa, huffing from their shoving match. "That's why we need to clear the air."

"Why didn't you tell me?" Choice ranted, stomping to all four corners of the room and back; her voice ripping like a jagged edge. "Why did you lie to me?"

"I had planned to tell you," Marian said weakly, "as soon as you graduated high school, but you beat me—"

"I wasn't trying to uncover your dirty, little secret." Choice flopped into the armchair. "I was only looking for my birth certificate. I needed it to complete my senior exit papers."

"I know—"

"How could I possibly know I'd find *two* birth certificates?"

"I know, Baby—"

"Don't!" Choice ripped. "Don't you dare call me *baby*!"

Marian's face creased. She changed the subject. "The funeral was nice."

"Good."

"All the relatives came home. It was like a family reunion."

"Good."

"Everybody asked about you, Choice."

"Oh, really? Did you bother to tell them the truth this time…that your dead sister, Maria, was *not* my aunt?"

Marian's voice sank. "Everybody knows."

Choice flailed her arms like a mad woman. "So, all my life, everybody knew that Maria was my *birth* mother and not my aunt; everybody, but me?"

"No. Not everybody, but it is common knowledge now." Marian consented.

Choice clutched her belly. It was raging like an inferno. "And does it make them want to throw up like it does me?"

"Please, Choice, let me explain." Marian's eyes mudded.

Choice slumped in her chair. "You can try."

"Your mom was married, Choice."

"Married? I never knew Aunt Maria…I mean…your sister was married."

"Well, she was. And she got pregnant with you."

"Okay—"

"Do you really want to hear all this?" Marian squirmed.

Choice's jaw cracked.

Marian exhaled with a gust. "You weren't her husband's baby."

"What?"

"No. Maria had…a lover, and she couldn't explain away the pregnancy—"

"Why not?"

"Because her husband, Laidlaw Dupree, had had a vasectomy five years earlier."

"Oh!"

"So, Laidlaw left her as soon as she started to show," Marian explained. "He got a divorce, and Maria took back her maiden name before you were born."

"So, who is my dad?" Choice gaped.

Marian King reset herself. Her frumpy black sack dress and black lace-up sneakers made her look like a frayed Humpty Dumpty. "I don't know if you've noticed, Choice, but I'm a plain woman," she said. "My sister, Maria, was the pretty one. And although I'm the eldest by two years, by the time you were born, I'd only had one serious boyfriend in my whole life…Carl Chancellor." She smiled weakly. "He was a quiet, gentle, handsome man, and he liked me. He really liked me. We were planning to get married."

"So what?"

"But Maria couldn't stand it." Marian's pulse raced. "She couldn't stand for me to have not even this one man for myself. She had to have him."

"Yeah, Maria was always a jealous-hearted—"

"And even though she was married to a beautiful man, Maria stole my Carl from me. She seduced him." Marian squeezed her eyes shut. "She said it was just that one time. She said it was to prove to me he didn't really love me; that he wasn't worthy of me. But I knew different." Marian's face sagged. "She ruined everything for me, for us. And in the process…she got pregnant—"

"Me?"

"Yes."

Choice finally allowed herself to breath. "So, where's my daddy, now?"

"Dead. He died in a car crash not long after you were born. They say he'd been drinking, but I never knew him to be a drinking man." Marian heaved. "Maria was trying to force him to marry her. Maybe the pressure just got to be too much for him."

"So why did you get involved with me?" Choice seized on the moment. "I was the baby that destroyed your future."

Shock registered on Marian's face. "Choice, don't you understand? I'd been praying for a family…a baby." She snuffed back her tears. "You were my one and only chance."

"But why did you cover for *her*?"

"Maria was my only sister, Choice. What else could I do but help her?"

"So, you helped her by lying to me for seventeen years!" Choice spat.

"It wasn't like that. Don't you see?" Marian pleaded. "When I got to the hospital two days after you were born, you were still in the nursery with 'Baby King' tagged to your wrist."

"Why?"

"Maria was devastated. She was a basket case. She was too depressed to even give you a name, and she was talking crazy, like she might kill herself…and you."

"What?"

141

"So, I did what I thought was right. Before it was filed, I convinced the nurse she'd misspelled the mother's name on your birth certificate." Marian tensed. "It wasn't hard since my name and my sister's are so much alike…she being Maria and me Marian."

"And then?"

"So, the nurse made you a new birth certificate with my name…mother, Marian King. And I slipped the old one into my pocket for safekeeping."

"And you kept them both?" Choice blared.

"I didn't mean to. I just couldn't find it in my heart to throw it away." Marian's head dropped. "But for your sake, I wish I had."

"And then what?"

"And then I named you…Choice. Because that's exactly who you are to me…my Choice."

"So, Maria just abandoned me?" Choice's defenses drooped.

"She was in no shape to take care of you." Marian raised her hands and let them flop down again. "Can't you see, Choice? She was a wreck. She couldn't handle the responsibility of raising a baby alone, and I could."

"So how did y'all pull it off?"

"She went home and said she'd had a miscarriage." Marian confessed. "And I went away for a while and came back with you. I told everyone I'd adopted you, and no one caught on for the longest time—"

"But when I started looking so much like Maria—"

"Yes." Marian nodded. "We were forced to tell the family members closest to us; the ones that noticed the resemblance."

Choice sagged. "But not me?"

"Choice your mom...Maria...was so embarrassed. Every time she looked at you it hurt her heart that she'd been so foolish as to bust up her perfectly good marriage...and hurt me in the process."

"So as usual, it was all about her!" Choice blared.

"Pretty much." Marian nodded. "But you know your aunt. That's just who she was. She couldn't help herself."

"Don't you mean...my *mom*?"

"Choice, I'm your mom. I've always been your mom, and that doesn't have to change. Can't you forgive me? I love you, Ba—" She reached for Choice's hand.

Choice snatched it back. "I've spent years trying to get over your lies. I don't know if I can ever forgive you."

"I know it's a lot to ask, Choice, but I've missed you so." Marian choked out the words. "And now that my sister's dead, I don't have anyone but you. Please give me another chance."

Choice's eyes turned beet red; her mind rolled back over her *dead* years on the street. "If only you knew what your lies have cost me."

"I'm sorry, Choice." Tears clogged Marian's voice. "I did what I thought was right at the time. I was trying to protect you and keep my sister's secret. It was so selfish of us…me and Maria. It hurt you deeply, and I'm so, so sorry."

Choice hopped to her feet. "I can't do this anymore." She stabbed at the door. "Leave!"

"But I've come all this way from Nashville," Marian pleaded. "Can't you find it in your heart to spend even a little time with me?"

"I don't have a heart. Don't you remember?" Choice swung open her front door. "You broke it into a million pieces a long time ago."

Marian pushed up off the couch. "I understand, and I won't trouble you anymore." Her heavy feet shuffled to the door. "But know this, Choice." Her voice choked with tears. "You might've been switched at birth, but I'm your Mother-in-Love. I chose you back then, and I'd choose you over again and again. You are, and always will be, my sweet, little baby girl."

Choice slammed the door on her past. Hot tears were streaming like molten lava before she could stumble into her bed.

# CHAPTER 18: SPEAK NOT EVIL OF ONE ANOTHER.

*James 4:11*

Assistant Pastor Sensay Logan could hardly sit still in the pulpit on Sunday morning. He couldn't focus on Pastor Mayberry's sermon, and not even Johnesther's nasty little side-bar comments could faze him. He didn't see Choice in the congregation, and he was concerned. *She never misses 11 o'clock service.*

He saw Mother Brown sitting with the senior women. There was Laqueeta and her fidgety boys on the back row. Rachael and her son, Jake, had their heads together with Gabbi on the second row. Angel, looking quite the charmer with her dark hair flowing and cleavage exposed, was sitting with her parents in their usual spot. A very haggard-looking Fancy was camped out on the front row in sniffing distance of Evangelist Mayberry. If Sensay didn't know better, he'd say those were bags under Sis. Fancy's bloodshot eyes.

*But no Choice.* Every time the doors opened Sensay craned his neck to see if she would be amongst the latecomers. *That's it!* He fumed. *If she doesn't get here before the end of service, I'm breaking all the W.O.O.F. rules. I'm going to her house.*

****

Johnesther couldn't wait until they got home from service that Sunday. She hit Pastor Mayberry with it while they were still in the car. "Mayberry," she said, lips smacking, "the Lord has given me a great vision!"

"Johnesther, Baby, can it wait 'til tomorrow." The pastor groaned. "The Spirit was so high today; I'm a bit drained."

"But, honey, you don't have to do a thing but listen," she schmoozed. "I'll do all the talking."

"I bet." The pastor braced himself. "Let's hear it."

"I understand we need to get our membership numbers up—"

"Where'd you hear that?" Pastor Mayberry frowned.

"Uhh...I don't know...probably overheard some of the deacons talking." Johnesther winced. "But here's the idea."

"Okay."

"We need to go to two services."

"Two services?"

"Yes. We could double our membership that way in a very short while."

"Johnesther, we only have about 200 regular members. Our sanctuary seats 500. The one service we have now is less than half full."

"I know, but that's the beauty of going to two services," Johnesther said cheerfully. "If we had 200 regular members in each service, our numbers would double overnight."

"But, honey, we're building a family at Overcoming Faith. A family has to pray and worship together to grow strong. That's why the New Testament church had such mighty power—"

"New Testament Church? What New Testament Church?" Evangelist Mayberry mocked. "Is it competing for our members?"

Pastor Mayberry squinted at her incredulously. "It's in the Book of Acts…you know…the Bible—"

"But Mayberry, each one of the services will be like its own family. You can handle first service. I'll handle second service. And Sensay can handle both services on fifth Sundays."

"Sensay is the Assistant Pastor." Pastor Mayberry sighed. "So, why're you limiting him to fifth Sundays?"

"He's not worthy of handling any service—"

"And why's that?"

"Because whether you know it or not, Mayberry, your precious Sensay is having an affair with one of your members, right under your nose."

"An affair?" The pastor balked. "With whom?"

"Choice King. Didn't you know?"

"I know that Sensay is very interested in Sis. King. He told me so himself. But they're not having an affair."

"Shows what you know!" Johnesther huffed. "They were spotted at a local restaurant…alone together…after y'all made this big deal about W.O.O.F. members not dating without chaperones."

"I don't know where you're getting your information, but if Sensay was with Choice you can rest assured Mother Brown knew all about it."

"Dating a member!" Johnesther sizzled. "That just proves we ought to put this Children's Education Building on hold—"

"Why?"

"Because it's obvious Sensay isn't mature enough to handle the responsibility; that's why! We could get the membership numbers up through the two services, first; and then we'd have enough money to build the new Children's wing for cash, later." Johnesther touched his hand. "And until this mess is cleared up with Sensay, Mayberry, I think I should preach the second service. He can handle fifth Sundays."

"But, honey, we're such a small congregation. It would be a shame to break us up where we wouldn't see each other every Sunday—"

"But how else will the church grow?" Johnesther steamed.

"Honey, we're building a church family, and that's more valuable than mere numbers."

"By any chance, Pastor, do you ever read or study the new trends?" Johnesther hissed. "Churches are growing because they're going to two and sometimes three services to accommodate the needs of the people in the community. That's the wave of the future."

"I do read, Johnesther, and I know that the benefits of a family environment and mutual support far outweigh sheer numbers—"

"But you've got some people who'd love to come to an 8 o'clock service right now, so they can go to work, or watch football, or shop, or whatever."

"But, Johnesther, when we get that new Children's Education Building that will bring in more parents and children and our numbers will grow."

"And what's the chance of that?" Evangelist Mayberry seethed. "These young parents might *send* their kids, but they're not coming to anybody's church!"

"Okay." Pastor Mayberry attempted to sidestep her growing fury. "When we grow our one service to the point we fill up those 500 seats, I'll be the first in line to expand to two services. But until then—"

"We haven't filled those 500 seats in all these years. That's why we need to come up with something new—"

"Or something old—"

"What?" Johnesther protested.

"Our church needs to stay together and pray about it."

"Mayberry, the Deacons and the Trustees want us to grow, and grow now." Johnesther flailed her hands. "Are you going against them?"

"No, I'm not going against them," the pastor said flatly. "This two-service idea isn't their idea. It's yours.

And I'm saying, what we would gain by two services…numbers…could be the very thing that could compromise what we've worked so hard to achieve…unity—"

"Whatever!" Johnesther lost it. "You're an old relic, Mayberry! You've lived past your time! You're an albatross around the church's neck. You're never going to be megachurch material—"

"Is that all you can think about, Johnesther?" Pastor Mayberry blared, his tongue stuffing more unspeakable words into his handsome jaw. "But I'm more concerned that we continue to operate like a family, rather than splitting us up into two services. We've just gotten to the point where we've started to trust each other and work together—"

"Hah! That's what you think!" Johnesther jumped out of the car and fled to the kitchen as soon as the garage door cracked open.

# CHAPTER 19: FORGIVE ONE ANOTHER.

*Colossians 3:13*

After Sunday service, Sensay fumbled around Oak Cliff until he found Choice's townhouse on Hunter's Trail. He parked on the curb and strolled up to the front door. He rang the doorbell. No answer. He rang it again. No answer. He ripped open the glass storm door and pounded on the wooden one. He could hear someone shuffling around inside. He waited a moment and then pounded again.

Finally, the door flew open. "What?" Choice croaked. Her voice sounded like the back side of the desert. Her hair was matted to her head, and she was wearing tattered sweats and horrid green slippers. She hadn't even bothered to wash her tear-stained face.

"You weren't at church—"

"And how's that any of your business?"

Sensay didn't wait for an invitation. He barged in. "I was just concerned about you."

"Get out!" Choice squeezed between clenched teeth. Weak from not eating or drinking, she spun on her heels and flopped onto the couch.

Sensay found his way into the kitchen, and he was also glad for what he didn't find—no drugs; no alcohol. Thankfully, he brought back a glass of water for her.

"Drink this," he demanded and sat down on the couch beside her.

Choice banged the untouched glass onto her vinyl coffee table and turned her head away from him. "Leave!"

"I'm not leaving until we talk."

"How dare you give my mom…my aunt…Marian my address."

"Choice, I'm sorry, but she called sounding so desperate. She said since you didn't come to your aunt's funeral, she needed to mail you some very important papers. She said you wouldn't return her calls so she needed your address. I'm your Assistant Pastor. What else could I—"

"You could mind your own business! Or better yet, you could've told me you gave that woman my address." Choice huffed. "She just showed up on my doorstep yesterday!"

"Choice, I'm very sorry." The assistant pastor reached for her hand. "I was going to tell you today…at church…but you never showed up."

Choice jerked her hand away and drew herself up into a tight ball. "No, I didn't come, and I may never come back. It's people like you that give *church* a bad name…busybody, do-gooders!"

"Please, drink your water, Choice." Sensay offered her the glass, again, and she refused. "I thought I was doing the right thing. After all, she's your family—"

"Family? Ha! Let me be the judge of that!"

"Help me out here, Choice. What's going on with you two?"

"You really want to know?" Choice's voice nearly failed. She picked up the glass and took a tiny sip.

"Yes, Choice. I really want to know."

Choice cleared her foggy throat and closed her eyes. "My senior year in high school I found out I had *two* birth certificates."

"Two?"

"Yes, at least that's how my life started." Choice gulped another sip. "The woman you talked to on the phone, Marian King, has been passing herself off as my mother since I was born, but—"

"But—" Sensay encouraged.

"But she's actually my aunt." Choice croaked. "My birth mom is the woman who died, and she'd been passing herself off as my aunt, until the day I found those two birth certificates."

"What happened when you found them?"

"Nothing!" Choice blared. "I didn't say a word to those two lying heifers! I just graduated high school and ran away the very same night."

"You ran away?"

"Are you crazy? Of course, I ran away!" By now, Choice was sobbing uncontrollably. "My whole life was a lie!" She wailed. "I had nobody. I had nothing. I had nowhere to go."

"So why didn't you stay and confront them?" Sensay reasoned.

"Why should I?" Choice shrugged tightly. "They'd just lie!"

"But how did you know?"

"Sensay, don't you understand!" Choice sniffed. "Up until then, I'd always wondered why the woman who was passing herself off as my aunt treated me so cold. I'd even asked…Marian…point blank: 'Why does your sister hate me so?'"

"And what did she say?"

"Nothing! She wouldn't even admit my feelings were valid. She just kept the lie going. All those years, Marian let me think she was my mom, and never did she ever let me know why my *real* mom hated me so." Choice wailed. "I guess every time she looked at me I reminded her of her big mistake…her guilt…her pain…and she took it all out on me!"

"Oh, Choice, I'm so sorry." Sensay reached out to hold her in his arms.

Choice balked. "What're you doing?" She pushed him back. "I don't like to be touched."

"Whoa!" Sensay raised his hands. "I just want to hold you until you feel better."

Choice eyed him cautiously. "Well, I guess that's okay."

Sensay moved in closer and circled her in his arms. He rocked her gently, like a two-year old.

"Don't you see, Sensay," Choice whimpered under his embrace. "All my life I thought it was my fault. I never felt good enough, or pretty enough, or worthy enough to earn her acceptance—" Choice crumbled into a heap in his lap. "Or her love."

"Ahh, Baby." Sensay caressed her cheek. "Please, don't cry. It's over now."

"Is it?" Choice popped up. "They ruined my life…the drugs—"

"So that's why you took up with those druggies?"

"They were the only ones who'd take me in," Choice mumbled. "They didn't judge me. They treated me like family. And before I knew it, I was doing what they did. I was taking drugs, too."

"It's only natural," Sensay said. "You were alone. You were scared—"

"I knew the things I was doing…the drugs I was taking…were going to kill me, but I couldn't stop. It was either, kill myself…or look up and live—"

"So that's when you found Jesus?" Sensay perked.

Choice wiped her eyes and a tiny smile leaked through. "Just think of it, Sensay. Out of all the filthy words on that nasty toilet wall the day I overdosed, only two of them jumped out at me: 'Jesus Saves'—"

"So, really, that's when Jesus found you?" Sensay finally understood.

"Yes." Choice nodded. "When I ended up in that rehab center instead of the morgue, I knew, without a doubt, Jesus saved me, and I wanted to get to know Him better."

"And that's why you came to Overcoming Faith."

"Yes." Choice scowled. "But now, it's all ruined."

"No, it's not, Choice." Again, the assistant pastor hugged her like a brother. "Jesus loves you. You don't have to run away anymore; not from your mother, or your aunt, or anybody. You're a child of the King...the King of Kings. You're in His family now...the family of life, not death."

"Oh, Sensay." Choice sobbed on his shoulder. "If only I could believe that. I've tried and tried to put the past behind me, but it keeps catching up with me—"

"And it will, until you quit running and stand your ground." Sensay insisted. "Stand on the Solid Rock."

"Jesus?"

"Yes, Choice. All of His promises are true. You can build a new life on them."

"But what about my mom...my aunt...Marian?"

"There's nothing you can do about that, Choice. Your mother was your mother, and your aunt is your aunt. It doesn't matter that you were switched at birth. You're here now, and I, for one, am very glad about it." He gently lifted her chin. "You can decide from this day forward to be free of all their lies and their mistakes."

Choice met his eyes. "But how?"

"You can forgive them." Sensay offered.

"Forgive?"

"Yes, Choice, let it go! Don't hold them to their mistakes. Regardless of what they did wrong, Marian did take care of you—"

"But I can't deal with her—"

"You have the right to choose what kind of relationship you have with your mom…your aunt…but you don't have to be a victim of their lies. You can build your own life…in Jesus."

"I can never call her, Mom, again."

"You don't have to."

"I can't call her Aunt…not now."

"You don't have to."

Choice's eyes drifted. "From now on, she'll just be plain, ole Marian."

"Choice, that's fine," Sensay said. "You can forgive her and love her as Marian."

"Love her?"

"Didn't Jesus love his enemies?"

"But—"

"Choice." Sensay caressed her face in both hands. "You've got to find a way," he said. "Please, don't let bitterness steal you away from me."

"But I don't know if I can," Choice whispered, her heart beating in sync with his.

"Baby, your life is a testimony," Sensay said tenderly. "People need to hear what Jesus can do in spite of what others did to you."

"Really?" Choice sniffed.

"Besides, Girl," Sensay said, and this time he hugged her like the man he hoped to be for her someday, "I've got much bigger plans for you."

# CHAPTER 20: BE AT PEACE WITH ONE ANOTHER.

*Romans 14:19*

The men had agreed to meet for lunch on Monday at the Longhorn Cafeteria on Westmoreland Avenue, which was a feat in itself since most pastors took Mondays off. They met behind closed doors in the community room. Until they'd had a chance to pow-wow, they didn't want their respective congregations to be any the wiser.

Pastor Mayberry and Assistant Pastor Sensay Logan were in attendance from Overcoming Faith. The head of the Deacon Board, J. C. Banks, and the president of the Trustees, Elroy Davis, from New Bethel Outreach had requested the meeting. New Bethel was located in the heart of South Oak Cliff, and they were widely respected for their outreach efforts to turn the tide on gang violence and teen pregnancies.

Deacon Banks closed the door to the private meeting room after they'd served themselves from the buffet. "Brothers, glad you could come." He nodded at Pastor Mayberry and Sensay. "Me and Bro. Davis, here, we've been kicking around an idea—"

"And we wanna see if it'll fly," Bro. Davis chimed in. He was the eldest member of the group and known to be a plain talker. The slight pouch in his jaw evidenced the pinch of chewing tobacco he kept lodged between his cheek and gum.

"Okay," Pastor Mayberry said flatly. "Let's get on with it." He was still a little jaded from the head-on collision he'd had with Johnesther the day before.

"We're very glad to be here." Sensay, the youngest man in the room, picked up the drooping mantle and ran with it. "It's truly an honor to meet with you," he said, taking his place next to Pastor Mayberry.

"Our churches are right 'round the corner from each other. It's a shame we ain't met 'fo now," Bro. Davis said. "And even with a church on every corner, looks like hell's 'bout to take over—"

"Elroy, we're here, now." Deacon Banks short-circuited his friend's tirade, since at his age he had a tendency to wander off point. "And we hope you'll be open to what we have to say."

"Go right ahead." Pastor Mayberry prompted.

"Well, first of all, you know we recently lost our pastor?"

"Yep, po' man dropped dead like a rock—"

"Yes," Pastor Mayberry said, "and we were very sorry to hear it. Our church prayed for his family and your congregation."

"Thank you." Deacon Banks groaned. "We're being sustained by the prayers of the saints."

"It's just a wonder any o' us still here." Brother Davis shifted his wad. "Death don't know no age no mo'—"

"Is there something in particular we can do for you?" Pastor Mayberry edged back in.

"First, let me say," Deacon Banks proceeded, "we have the highest regard for your ministry. You have a fine reputation for putting the Lord's word to work in the community."

"And you're doing great things at New Bethel, especially for our troubled teens." Sensay offered.

"And we know you to be a square shooter, Pastor Mayberry—"

"Brothers, I appreciate your vote of confidence." The pastor raised his hands. "And rest assured, the feeling is mutual, but where're you going with this?"

Deacon Banks took a deep breath. "We hear you're planning to build a new Children's Education Building; and, frankly, we want to get in on it."

"How so?"

"We wanna reach all the kids in our community...the churched and the un-churched."

"That's a very noble goal, but how will you go about it?" Pastor Mayberry said.

"Of course, we'd have to work out the details," Deacon Banks said, "but we want to join forces...partner with you...to get it done."

"That's right." Bro. Davis bobbed his head. "Get our two churches working on one accord."

"I'm open to the idea," Pastor Mayberry said, "anything to reach the children; but how would we do it?"

"You pay to build the building as planned," Deacon Banks said clearly, "and we'll help pay the monthly operating expenses…including Assistant Pastor Sensay's salary, staff salaries, and other operating expenses."

"Wow!" Sensay couldn't mask his enthusiasm. "Then we'd be able to build that much sooner and have our very own Children's Church."

"Work it, son!" Bro. Davis cheered him on. "It'll be like the day of Pentecost when the church had *all* things in common!"

"Yes," Deacon Banks smiled. "That's how we see it. The children from Overcoming Faith will be there, and New Bethel will funnel in children from all over the community through our outreach programs. There's no need for us to build two facilities when one will do."

"And working together, we can grow the membership in both of our churches—"

"And if we ever need to expand—"

"We'll work that out, too."

"It's so wonderful to meet brothers who aren't hung up on petty jealousies," Pastor Mayberry exclaimed.

"We ain't got time to pull against one another no mo'." Bro. Davis inserted. "Jesus is soon to return!"

"And we need to make sure our children are saved and able to lead happy, productive lives until then."

"Yeah, instead o' shootin' one another down like dogs in the street—"

"I can't wait to bring this before my leadership," Pastor Mayberry said. "I'm sure they'll agree wholeheartedly."

"Good," Deacon Banks said, "but there's just one more thing."

"Oh?"

"New Bethel is still in need of a pastor."

"I'm sure you're not eyeing my Assistant Pastor, over here." Pastor Mayberry smiled. "He's not available."

"No-siree." Bro. Davis laughed.

"But we would like for Evangelist Mayberry to consider becoming our new pastor," Deacon Banks said. "That is, if it's all right with you, Pastor Mayberry."

Pastor Mayberry's grin widened. "It's more than all right," he said. "I'm delighted for my wife to be blessed with this opportunity, and I'm sure she'll be honored to be considered."

"Let's be clear, "Deacon Banks said. "Evangelist Mayberry is being more than just considered."

"We hear she's a mighty fine preacher—"

"And we'd like to offer Evangelist Mayberry the position, as soon as possible." Deacon Banks concluded.

Pastor Mayberry slapped his thigh. "Then, my brothers, I'll discuss it with her right away and have her get in touch with you with her answer."

Brother Davis took the last word. "With you over there at Overcoming Faith and your wife with us at New

Bethel, we'll be like—" He scratched his bald head. "What's that y'all call them thangs, brothers?"

"Satellites!" The men exclaimed.

****

Meanwhile, Johnesther was pacing in Bliss' airport office. He'd ordered a catered lunch for just the two of them and let his secretary have the afternoon off.

"That's it, Bliss!" Johnesther blustered. "The very last straw!"

"Johnesther, calm down and talk to me."

"First, I tried to get that fool, Mayberry, to let me be Co-Pastor; no go! Then we tried to get those fool deacons to go for a satellite church in North Dallas; no go! And now I've tried to get Mayberry to go to two services so we can drive up our membership numbers—"

"And—"

"No go!" Johnesther thudded into the seat across from Bliss.

"Hmm." Bliss needled. "If the man you're married to won't hear you, Girl; you ain't got yo'self nothin'."

"Mayberry just doesn't get it!" Johnesther blazed. "He doesn't get it! And it took all I had not to lay my religion down and bless that man out where he stood!"

Bliss grinned. "Well, sometimes you just gotta do what you gotta do to get that monkey off yo' back—"

"That ignorant, short-sighted, mealy-mouthed man makes me so furious I could just scream!" Johnesther stomped in her pumps.

"I hear ya." Bliss drawled. "So, what you gonna do about it?"

"I'm filing for divorce as soon as I can get me a lawyer—"

"Divorce?"

"Yes! And you're going to do the same."

"Divorce Marvella?"

"Sure. You've been sick of that big woman for years." Johnesther raked him over with her eyes. "Besides, word is you've got your eye on a little honey in W.O.O.F. anyhow."

Bliss' cool cracked. "Who told you that?"

"A little birdie." Johnesther snickered, enjoying seeing him squirm. "What does it matter? It's time for us to move on to Plan B."

"Which is?"

"Take the money and run!" The evangelist said flatly.

Bliss chuckled. "So, First Lady, you're ready to start your own church in North Dallas?"

"Most definitely! I'll be...well...I'm having a major birthday soon, and I'm running out of time to fulfill my God-given purpose."

"You sure you don't want to wait for the satellite church idea to catch hold with the Deacon Board?" Bliss cautioned. "I've been pushing it real hard with them and the Trustees, too. The men seem to be coming around to our way of thinking."

"I've been working the senior women, too, Bliss, but it's no use." Johnesther fumed. "That Flora Brown has entirely too much influence over them!"

"Mother Brown? How so?"

"She's got those ole biddies convinced that loyalty to the Pastor outweighs our brilliant outreach stats for the satellite church."

"But—"

"Forget it Bliss! Those pea-brained folks will never give us the power we need to make it happen." Johnesther huffed. "I'm sick of waiting. And I'm sick of Mayberry and his *can't-do* attitude most of all!"

"Then I'll file for divorce." Bliss shrugged. "We can use the same lawyer." He considered. "What about that young filly from W.O.O.F.?"

"Fancy? Oh, no! She hasn't even passed the bar." Johnesther sniffed. "Besides, she's a little too nosy for my taste. She's been all up in my face trying to get on as the church's managing attorney. But I really don't trust that girl."

"Why not?"

"She's a cunning little minx; I'll give her that. But she's a real power junkie." Johnesther scowled. "A wacky train-wreck waiting to happen, just like her crazy mamma who died in the nut house. I will *never* do business with that girl—"

"Okay-okay, I get it. Then who do we get?" Bliss pressed.

"Somebody outside the church, of course. I'll come up with somebody by tomorrow. Don't worry; I want those papers filed so we can move the Annex Fund over into our own account."

"Tell me again why you think Pastor won't press charges against us when he finds out we've taken the money?" Bliss stammered.

"Charges?" Johnesther sneered. "Why, Bliss, we're doing the Lord's work, and they'll be too embarrassed to admit how gullible they were."

"Oh, really?"

"Besides, how can they possibly not want to sow financially into the mission of planting an exciting, new church in North Dallas?" Johnesther surmised. "After all, we'll be sister churches, even if we had to push them along a little. Plus, Mayberry is the forgiving sort. You know that."

"I hear you, Johnesther, but this is money we're talking about…big money."

"Bliss, we can make up that paltry, little $3 million in less than six months when our megachurch gets off the ground. Don't forget; we'll be up in North Dallas where people have mon-ey. The tithes will come rolling in—"

"Yeah, but what if they *do* file charges?" Bliss quavered.

"Don't worry. It would be tied up in court so long, we'd be able to pay back Overcoming Faith—" She snapped her fingers. "With interest!"

"So, how're you going to handle the Pastor until we've filed for divorce?"

"I'll give him the cold shoulder, of course," Johnesther said smoothly. "When he's in, I'll be out. I'll plan my schedule so I won't have to see him at all. And I'll be snoring by the time he hits the bed."

"Johnesther, you're a woman of action. I'll give you that." Bliss chuckled. "But are you sure you want to go through with this?"

"I've never been surer of anything in my life." The evangelist clucked her tongue. "*You* just don't get cold feet."

"Not hardly." Bliss blustered. "I ain't got nothin' to lose by divorcing Marvella. The marriage's been dead for years. Besides," he crooned, "it could land me one step closer to you."

"You just never know, Bliss." Johnesther sugar-coated her voice and put a little extra pepper in her strut. She stopped at the door and shot him a backward glance, holding her prized legs at just the right angle. "I'll call you tomorrow."

# CHAPTER 21: ADMONISH ONE ANOTHER.

*Colossians 3:16*

Deacon Bliss' secretary had left for the day after summoning Rachael to his church office. Rachael approached his door with some reluctance; although, she felt fairly safe since the Wednesday night W.O.O.F. meeting would be starting soon. It would give her good cause to cut her meeting with the deacon short. Mustering up her courage, she tapped on his door.

"Well, come in," Bliss said, snapping to attention when he saw Rachael standing there. His cordial manner was bested only by his big smile. "Come on in here, Pretty Lady."

"I only have a few minutes," Rachael sputtered. "I'm headed to the W.O.O.F. meeting, and Mother Brown is expecting me to give a full report on our Investment Club."

"I know." Bliss sat back down behind his desk. "Just take a seat, and I'll get you there in plenty o' time." He winked. "Promise."

"You seem rather pleased with yourself tonight," Rachael said, sitting on the edge of her seat. She held her purse against her breast like a shield.

"I am, Baby." His eyes sparked. "I'm so excited. I should have done this years ago."

"Done what?"

Bliss moved around the desk and propped on the edge nearest Rachael. "Promise me you won't tell a soul."

"Huh?" Rachael fidgeted with her locket. His strange mood was making her nervous. "Does this have something to do with our Investment Club?"

"Don't worry about the Club." He patted the thick manila folder on his desk. "I've got that handled. It only needs y'all's signatures, and it's good to go."

"Then what?"

"Promise?"

"Okay. Sure."

Deacon Bliss leaned in closer. "I'm divorcing Marvella as soon as I can get a lawyer lined up."

Rachael nearly jumped out of her chair. "You're what?"

"Shhh." Bliss smiled. "I told you I'd fix it for us to be together—"

"*Us?* There's no *us.*" Rachael blinked. "I want nothing to do with you leaving your wife." She scrambled for the exit, but Bliss pressed her shoulders back down into the seat.

"Don't leave now." The deacon moaned. "I need you. Don't you know that? I need you to be my woman…my wife."

"No way!" Rachael clutched her locket. "Just show me where to sign these papers, and I'm long gone."

"But Baby, you're not seeing the big picture. I can give you the finer things in life…you and little man." He blew his hot breath in her ear. "And then you can have my babies—"

"Babies!" Rachael pushed him aside. "Deacon, you've lost your mind!" She snatched up the manila folder and ran for the door.

Deacon Bliss beat her to it and blocked her way. He gripped her shoulders in his strong, chocolate hands. "Don't you have any feelings for me at all?"

Rachael held up her locket, like it was an amulet to ward off evil spirits. "Move!" she demanded.

Bliss chuckled. "Girl, you should see yourself now. You've got that hot blood; the kind I like." He pried her hand away from her locket. "Why're you always fooling around with this thing? Who've you got squirreled away in there?"

"None of your business!"

"Ahh, Baby, let me see." Bliss teased. "I promise I'll let you go, for now, if you'll let me take just one little peek."

Rachael sized him up. "Okay, and then I'm gone." She clutched the file under one arm, and with her free hand, she snapped open the locket.

Bliss drew in closer, pinning her against the door with the full weight of his desire. He took the locket in hand. "What's this?" He dropped it like a hot iron. "Who?"

Rachael swerved her body from under him. "My son. My mamma," she said. "Why?"

"What's her name?" Bliss sputtered, stricken.

"Why?"

"Her name?" He flared. "Give me the woman's name!"

"Eureka. Eureka Jones." Rachael scowled. "What's it to you?"

Bliss staggered back and bounced into his desk chair. "Yo' mamma?" His eyes spun the color wheel from red to purple and back again. "Eureka Jones?"

It was the way he said her mother's name that final time. Rachael knew. She stared at Deacon Bliss; the way the lamp light shadowed his face, and she knew. At that moment, she realized it was the profile he shared with her very own son. She'd never noticed it before, but now it was crystal clear. Deacon Raython Bliss was drawn to her because he was her long, lost daddy. And she knew, for the very first time, he knew it, too. If Eureka Jones was her mother, Raython Bliss knew he was her daddy.

Rachael opened the door quietly and left with the Investment Club file jammed under her arm.

****

On the other end of the hallway, Choice ran into Laqueeta prior to the W.O.O.F. meeting. She let her have it with both barrels. "I hear you tricked poor Gabbi into taking care of your boys this past weekend!" Choice blared.

"That's none of yo' business, Trick!" Laqueeta twirled a polka-dotted fingertip in her face. "Who you s'ppose to be, huh, the po-po? Who you; the soul po-lice up in here?"

Choice pushed her finger aside. "No, but maybe the others can't see through you; I can. I've seen plenty of users like you on the streets."

"User? Huh!" Laqueeta stepped to Choice again. "I have you know, Gabbi's got plenty free time since she gave up *cheerleading*—"

"That's not the point!"

"And she needs to get away from that weird roommate o' hers just as bad as I need to get away from them bad boys o' mine."

"Angel?"

"Yeah, yo' girl, Angel. Her li'l halo be slippin'—"

"Leave Angel out of this!" Choice blared. "This is about *you* taking advantage of Gabbi so that *you* could run off with some man."

Laqueeta went nose to nose with Choice. "I ain't never told nobody I wasn't gonna have me a man."

"Yes, you did." Choice's eyes locked on her. "By joining W.O.O.F., you agreed to serve and lay off sex."

"Humph!" Laqueeta stepped off, hands on hip. "I see it, now. You're just jealous, Girl, 'cause my man takes me places…Vegas, South Beach, Rodeo Drive—"

"And why should I be jealous of the likes of you, Laqueeta? You're just a low-down user."

"Uh-huh!" Laqueeta snatched off one earring and then the other. "Nobody talks to me like that and gets away—"

"I'll talk to you anyway I please," Choice boomed, "until you quit using us up and spitting us out!"

"Me? Me?" Laqueeta whined. "You don't say nothing when Gabbi keeps Rachael's little boy...Jake!"

"That's because Rachael and Gabbi have a *real* relationship. Rachael's smart. She's helping Gabbi graduate!"

"Then what about Fancy? What about Angel? They don't help nobody!"

"Fancy's up to her neck in law school, and Angel's a serious student-athlete." Choice defended. "They're doing good if they can even make the meetings."

"That's what you think!" Laqueeta grinned wickedly. "Ever since Gabbi got saved, Angel, *yo' serious student-athlete*, she's been bangin' every one o' them dudes on that football team—"

"Shut your lying mouth, Laqueeta!" Choice's nostrils flared. "You can't turn this around. I saw you sneaking on the church grounds with some man! I ought to tell Mother Brown—"

"Then why don't ya?" Laqueeta's eyes blazed.

"Because it's not about you!" Choice fired. "It's about your poor, little boys—"

"Ladies!" Mother Brown walked between the two women. "Don't you have something better to do than loud talk each other out here in the hallway?" Her tone felt like a tug on a schoolboy's ear. "Is this how you want to represent W.O.O.F?"

"Sorry, Mother Brown." Laqueeta replaced her earrings. "We just don't see eye-to-eye…about the Investment Club; ain't that right, Choice?"

"Sure."

"Then let's discuss it inside at our meeting, like sisters; shall we?" Mother Brown led the way.

****

Fancy would be a little late coming to the W.O.O.F. meeting because she had to make an urgent call on her new smartphone. "Like I said, I'm sorry to bother you, Evangelist, but this can't wait until our next lunch."

"You're not disturbing me, Fancy, dear. Church business is always important business. Go on—"

"A little while ago, I overheard Deacon Bliss telling Rachael he was going to divorce his wife so he could marry her—"

"You heard what?" Johnesther's phone nearly flew out of her hand.

"I told you I'd keep an eye on things. I saw Rachael go into his office, and I followed her."

"And you heard Bliss tell Rachael he was getting a divorce?" Johnesther flapped. "That girl could ruin us!"

"Don't worry. I don't think she'll tell anybody."

"Why not?"

"He swore her to secrecy, and Rachael's one to keep her word."

"Did the deacon happen to mention any other members…getting a divorce, I mean?" The evangelist angled.

"No. Who?"

"Oh, it's nothing." Johnesther said skillfully. "I just wondered if we had an epidemic on our hands."

"No. I don't think—"

"Did Rachael seem interested in his marriage proposal?" Johnesther softened.

"No, but he sure did sound determined…at least until the subject of her locket came up."

"Locket? What locket?" Johnesther quizzed.

"I couldn't see his face, but he got awfully quiet after he saw the picture of Rachael's mom hidden in her locket.

"Her mother?" Johnesther flapped.

"Eureka Jones."

"Well, maybe seeing her mom like that made Bliss realize how young Rachael really is," Johnesther said.

"Yeah, he's got her by at least twenty years—"

"Her mother is probably more our…his age." Johnesther mused.

Fancy snickered. "And with Rachael's mother being dead and all, maybe the old skirt-chaser came face to face with his own mortality."

"Anyhow, thank you Fancy for bringing this to my attention." Johnesther recovered from the shock. "I'm sure I don't have to tell you how vital it is to keep this as sacred as you would…any other attorney-client confidence."

"Just a few more months of law school, then the bar, and then—"

"Yes, yes, Fancy. I'm keenly aware of your career plans." Johnesther checked her tone. "And of course, my dear, I'll keep your ambitions in mind."

"Then you'll have no worries from me." Fancy squeezed her temples to contend with a throbbing migraine. The growing pressures of her grueling schedule and mounting debt were making it harder to keep her pesky nerves in check. "I…I know how to keep my mouth shut."

"I'll try to talk some sense into Deacon Bliss tomorrow, and maybe this'll all go away—"

"He can't spoil everything." Fancy's hand shook. "We just can't let him spoil everything—"

"Goodnight, Fancy."

# CHAPTER 22: EDIFY
## ONE ANOTHER.

*I Thessalonians 5:11*

When Fancy got off the phone with Evangelist Mayberry, she eased into the W.O.O.F. meeting which was already in progress.

Mother Brown was saying, "Let's admit it, sisters, we've all been hurt…by something or somebody."

Laqueeta's eyes rolled up to the ceiling. *You got that right, Mamma! I hurt every time them dead-beat dads don't send me no money for they boys!*

Angel's eyes sank to the floor. *I don't get it. I got my wish. I'm hooking up with all the guys. Nobody ignores me anymore! So why do I feel so…sad?*

Gabbi's face blushed scarlet. *It's like totally rad! I do feel better since I quit hooking up with all those guys. But Angel took my place…and that like totally sucks!*

Rachael's nerves marched up her back and tied a knot around her throat. *Man! Can it get any worse? My long-lost daddy…Raython Bliss! My mamma…dead! And me…just one more baby-mamma drama!*

Choice's seat heated up like a griddle. *Do I hurt? Of course, I hurt! How can I not hurt? My mom tossed me out like a sack of trash. My aunt fed me nothing but lies. What's left?*

Fancy raked a shaky hand through her tousled braids. *Sure; I used to hurt…until I learned to hurt the other guy first. Hmph! Now, it's my payday time!*

"I can see we're all giving this some serious thought," Mother Brown continued. "Perhaps the scriptures can help."

The group stared at her blankly.

"Will somebody please read, Colossians 2:10?"

Choice flipped to the passage in her Bible and read, "Ye are complete in Him—"

"Stop right there." Mother Brown instructed. "Now, someone read, Ephesians 1:6."

Unlike Fancy, the articulate one, she stammered through every word. "He hath made us…accepted…in the…Beloved."

"Do you see it, ladies?" Mother Brown said. "When you trusted Jesus to save you, He not only forgave you, but He also made you *complete* and *accepted*. Jesus made you whole! And at some point, knowing who you are in Jesus has got to be enough."

"Huh?"

"God's love is not just some words on paper." Mother Brown hoisted up her Bible. "Jesus died for you and left you His Spirit so you can *feel* how much He loves you."

"Then why don't we feel it?" Gabbi quipped.

"Because we'd rather believe the world's lie than the Lord's truth." Mother Brown affirmed.

"What lie?"

"The lie that you're worthless, needy, all alone; that you've got to use shortcuts to find happiness; that you've got to look for love from all the wrong people." Mother Brown gripped the makeshift podium, trying to shake off the image of her darling Lily—bruised and broken.

"So, what's the truth?"

Mother Brown reset her thick lenses and gave them a look. "The truth is you are *complete* and *accepted* in Jesus."

"But we've got real problems, right here and now—"

"Of course, you do," Mother Brown rebutted, "but at some point, knowing the truth must become more real, more precious to you, than the hurt you feel, or the people who cause it."

"But how?"

"You can change your mind!" Mother Brown contended. "Let go of the lie and grab hold of the truth. You...are...loved!"

"But how do you deal with the people who hurt you?"

Mother Brown pursed her lips. "You forgive them."

"Forgive?" Rachael blared. "The ones who mess over us?"

"Yes." Mother Brown nodded. "In God's eyes, we're no better than the people who hurt us...but He forgave us; didn't He?"

"Now, Mother Brown, come on." Laqueeta broke in. "On the for real side tho', you trying to tell us you forgave that dude what shot your baby girl down in cold blood?"

"Laqueeta!"

"What? I'm just sayin'—"

"Yes." Mother Brown removed her glasses and wiped her eyes. "I had to."

"But why?"

"How?"

Mother Brown reseated her frames. "As long as I hated him, I was blocked up. I was dead inside. Do you know what I mean?" She gazed at them from one to the other. "And nobody's worth that. I had to forgive him so I could feel the love of Jesus flowing through me again." Her voice settled over them like angel's wings. "Don't you see? The joy of the Lord is all I've got. Jesus is my life."

"Oh?"

Mother Brown smiled a knowing smile. "Until we *trust* Jesus and *believe* we're precious to Him, we can't move forward, or form healthy relationships—"

"Like with guys?" Gabbi giggled.

"Or with our children." Choice flashed at Laqueeta.

"Whatever, Trick!" Laqueeta shot back.

Mother Brown stood between them to preserve the solemnity of the moment. "Or it may be a ministry opportunity—"

"Or a career opportunity," Fancy said, ever mindful of the deal she had cooking with Evangelist Mayberry.

"But none of these good things can come our way until we put the past behind us and give to others what Jesus has so freely given to us…forgiveness, love, hope…someone to trust."

*Forgiveness?* Choice mouthed to herself.

Mother Brown clasped her hands together. "So tonight, ladies, let's take a moment and let it all go...the pain, anger, bitterness, disappointment; our failures and the failures of others. Let's put it behind us, once and for all, and move forward."

A stillness fell over the room like a giant cosmic vortex, sucking up every painful experience that was being released.

Rachael sobbed softly. Choice prayed audibly. Gabbi smiled uncontrollably. And Mother Brown just folded her arms and rocked.

Laqueeta, Angel and Fancy looked on, astonished.

Mother Brown would never forget that night. For out of the fire of their praise, Choice rose up like a phoenix to share her testimony with the group for the first time. She walked to the front of the room and said, "Hello, my name is Choice. I'm a recovering drug addict, and I was switched at birth."

With that, the W.O.O.F. members started working their church fans overtime.

Of course, Choice saw the question marks register in their eyes, but she was not dissuaded. Had she been able to see the thoughts in their minds, however, she might have kept her true confessions to herself; especially the sordid details of her life—*BC* (before Christ).

*TMI!* Laqueeta's mind raced. *Here this Trick is trying to act like she's better than me, and all the time she's just a messed up ole crack-ho! I'm just sayin'—*

*CHA-CHING!* Fancy straightened in her seat. *Another valuable nugget to keep Evangelist Mayberry solidly on my team!*

*OMG!* Gabbi's eyes flashed like tambourines. *I'm like totally surprised! Our own little Choice…on the streets?*

*MAN!* Rachael sagged. *Just when you think you've got it bad, somebody else steps up and takes your place—big time!*

*WOW!* Angel's chest flooded with envy. *At least she's got a life. That's more than I can say for myself!*

If their slack jaws and pin-pointed pupils were any indication, everyone in the room was suffering from a mild case of shock. As such, Mother Brown was probably the only one to hear Choice's closing comment.

"And, now," Choice said firmly, "it's up to me to make sure I never mess up again."

With that, Mother Brown closed the meeting. She gave Choice a tight squeeze and a warm whisper. "Come by my house tomorrow. Let's have lunch; okay?"

"Okay." Choice nodded and sagged back to her seat, feeling as flimsy as a purged soul could be.

# CHAPTER 23: PRAY FOR ONE ANOTHER.

*James 5:16*

After such a soul-stirring W.O.O.F meeting, Rachael made sure she was at the end of the line forming around Mother Brown. It was urgent that she speak with her, but she didn't want the others to overhear.

When it was her turn, Mother Brown patted her on the back. "Great job, Rachael! That work you did with Deacon Bliss got our Investment Club off the ground. Everyone was very excited about your report tonight."

Rachael's eyes bugged out. "Oh, thanks."

"Are you all right?"

"We *need* to talk—"

"Then you and Jake come by the house tonight. We…I have a surprise for you."

"And, *oh-oh*," Rachael retorted, "do I have a surprise for you!"

\*\*\*\*

When Rachael and little Jake arrived at Mother Brown's, Tyrone was already there.

Jake jumped into his daddy's arms without a word.

"What're you doing here?" Rachael quizzed.

"He's your surprise," Mother Brown said.

"What?" Rachael protested. "I don't understand."

"Have you forgotten?" Mother Brown smiled. "Your birthday is Friday, and Tyrone has some great news."

"Oh?" Rachael stiffened. She needed to talk to Mother Brown without delay.

"Tell her Tyrone." Mother Brown prompted.

Tyrone held Rachael's hand and sat her down at the dining room table. "I completed my mechanics certificate last week, and I've got a great job lined up at the Lexus dealership next week!"

"That's great," Rachael said flatly, still itching to talk to Mother Brown.

"Aren't you excited?" Tyrone pressed.

"Sure, Tyrone, I'm real excited for you."

"Excited for us." Tyrone jockeyed for her attention. "This means I'll be able to help out more with Jake's expenses—"

"Oh? Child support? Okay. That'll help."

"Tell her the rest." Mother Brown needled.

Tyrone's enthusiasm was dampened by Rachael's cool reception. "I also moved into my own apartment," his voice hollowed. But that news flash got Rachael's attention.

"You left your parents?" Rachael sparked.

"Yep, thanks to Mother Brown," Tyrone explained. "She fronted me the money, and I'll pay her back out of my first check."

"That sure was nice of you, Mother Brown." Rachael smiled. "So, the two of you've been scheming behind my back, huh?"

Mother Brown's eyes twinkled through her heavy lenses. "More like strategizing."

"But Tyrone," Rachael said tenderly, "what about your mom?"

"She's upset. Dad's upset." Tyrone shrugged. "But if I'm going to be a man, I've got to get out on my own."

"I'm so proud of you, Tyrone." Rachael's heart softened, sensing his need for her trust. "I know it took a lot for you to do this."

"I wanted to do the right thing for us, Rachael, for you and Jake." He pulled her up from her chair and planted a warm kiss on her lips. Rachael wrapped her arms around his sagging waistline and rested her head on his shoulder. Jake swung on his daddy's pants leg.

Mother Brown excused herself to the kitchen. It was time to bring out the birthday cake and ice cream.

# CHAPTER 24: BEAR ONE ANOTHER'S BURDENS.

*Galatians 6:2*

On Thursday, the fateful day after the W.O.O.F. meeting had been blasted on all sides by revelations and true confessions, Johnesther couldn't wait to get her fangs into Bliss. She blistered him as soon as her feet landed in his plush airport office.

"What's your problem?" Evangelist Mayberry stormed. "Can't you keep it in your pants long enough for us to get our hands on that *Annex Fund*?"

Bliss hopped up and shut the door. "Johnesther, keep your voice down! You can't come busting up in my office like this! Who you think you talkin' to?"

"I'm talking to you...you pervert...messing with Rachael Jones." Johnesther shrilled. "That little girl is young enough to be your daughter!"

Bliss froze. "What's that?"

"How dare you tell her you're getting a divorce!" Johnesther flamed. "That's supposed to be our little secret. Remember?"

"Who told you?"

"I've got my sources."

"Was it Rachael?" Bliss scrambled.

"No! Apparently, she's got more discretion in the matter than you!"

"Then who?" Bliss pressed.

"Does it matter?" Johnesther brought her voice to a scathing whisper. "All that matters is that you keep your mouth shut until both of us can file for divorce and get our hands on that *Annex Fund*. Without it, we won't be able to start my new church in North Dallas. Is that clear?"

Bliss pointed her to a chair, and they both plopped down. "Of course, it's clear, Johnesther. No need to get all riled up about it. Nobody knows—"

"When anybody knows, everybody knows; and we can't afford that right now. Understood?"

"Yes, ma'am." Bliss grinned in an attempt to regain control of the situation.

"Anyway." Johnesther blew out a gust and crossed her legs. "I've got a lawyer lined up for us. She's just waiting on your call." She shoved the lawyer's business card across his desk. "Call her today, and let's get on with this before the cat's out of the bag."

"You're right; my bad." Bliss granted her a conciliatory smile. "But you don't have to worry anymore. I'm done with that Rachael-Jones girl."

"Are you sure?"

"That briar is from under my saddle...sho-nuff!"

"Why should I believe you, Bliss?"

"Huh? I thought you knew." The deacon peeked out of his office door and closed it back again. "I thought that's why you were so blame mad."

"What is it, Bliss?" Johnesther fumed. "I don't have a clue what you're talking about."

"Oh?" Bliss kicked his boots upon his desk. "Then never mind."

"Stop with the drama, Bliss." Johnesther flared. "There can be no secrets between us. Tell me!"

"Oh, all right." The deacon planted his boots back on the floor. "You see, I looked in that locket that Rachael-girl wears around her neck—"

"And—"

"And...it's a picture of her mamma—"

"Eureka Jones." Johnesther supplied. "Yeah, I know."

"You know?" Bliss flapped. "What do you know?"

"Nothing, Bliss. Go on!"

"You see, me and Eureka had a...thang...back in the day."

Johnesther gasped. "Are you trying to tell me Rachael Jones is your own kid?"

"I knew the woman had a baby girl for me, but I didn't stick around to get caught up in the drama." Bliss admitted. "I ran off and married Marvella just to keep my distance from that crazy cow."

"Oh, my God, Bliss!" Johnesther's amazement eroded into laughter. "You must feel like the biggest fool alive, trying to get it on with your own daughter."

Bliss' face caved. "Don't rub it in, Johnesther. I feel bad enough as it is."

"Good. And hopefully Rachael won't tell the world what a fool you are before we can move the Annex Fund from the church's bank account to our bank account."

"Rachael ain't gonna tell a soul." Bliss scowled. "She don't want nobody to know I'm her daddy."

"I have half a mind to get you to move the Annex Fund to our bank account today—"

"Hold yo' horses!" Bliss raised his hand. "We can't do that. We can't show our hand too soon."

"Why not?"

Bliss set his eyes on Johnesther. "Don't you understand? We can't have the withdrawal showing up on the church's monthly bank statement before our divorce papers are filed."

Johnesther gasped. "Of course, Bliss. You're right."

"Come on, Suga, don't go worrying yo' pretty little head none. I'm just like the undertaker—"

"What?"

"I'll be the last one to let you down," Bliss said, adding a cheesy grin.

Johnesther couldn't resist rewarding him with a little smile. "All right then," she said, "we'll file our divorce papers tomorrow...and I suggest we skip church on Sunday."

"But Sunday is Mother's Day—"

"And what do you care?"

"Yeah, I see yo' point." Bliss conceded. "Besides, I wouldn't be caught dead at Overcoming Faith. I ain't ready to run into that Rachael-girl again."

Johnesther placed a dramatic hand across her forehead. "So, in that case, I feel a terrible migraine coming on."

"I heard that!" Bliss grinned.

"And if there's no fallout about your impending divorce," Johnesther said, mounting a miraculous recovery, "we'll know we're in the clear."

"Yeah, if them buzzards at Overcoming Faith ain't picking over my bones by Sunday, then we'll know Rachael didn't spill the beans."

Johnesther nodded her agreement. "And next week, I'll move out into a luxury hotel."

Bliss raised his brows. "Got room for two, *Sis. Legs*?" He greased his chops. "I may need a little...consoling."

"If you're a good boy, Bliss," Johnesther said in her most seductive tone, "there's just no telling what could happen."

\*\*\*\*

Choice took the afternoon off to have a leisurely lunch with Mother Brown, as requested. Choice was sure her testimony at the W.O.O.F. meeting the previous evening had taken them all by complete surprise, and she wanted Mother Brown's honest reaction. However, she didn't realize until she was standing on her front steps that the prospect of their encounter would make her knees feel like running water.

Iris, nearly two years old, was making funny faces at Choice from behind the storm door while she was gathering up the courage to ring the doorbell.

Mother Brown rushed to the door to catch up with her frisky granddaughter. "Oh, hi, Choice." She laughed. "Didn't know you were here. I see Miss Iris has been entertaining you."

"Cute as a button, like always," Choice said. When she stepped inside, Iris leapt into her arms. Surprisingly, that gave her knees some relief.

"Bring that heavy load on in here," Mother Brown teased, "and let's have our lunch at the dining room table."

Ever so gently, Choice settled Iris into her booster chair.

Mother Brown offered them an array of cold salads and warm, crusty bread. They could hear each other chewing in the awkward silence. Finally, Mother Brown took the lead. "Thank you, Choice, for sharing your story with us last night; I know it wasn't easy, especially on the eve of Mother's Day."

"No, it wasn't easy," Choice admitted, "but it was good to get it out in the open once and for all."

"I heard what you said at the end, too." Mother Brown crunched her bread. "That's why I wanted to talk to you."

"Not the drugs and my crazy upbringing?"

"Nope, I understand that." Mother Brown glimmered. "We all make mistakes of one sort or another, but how we choose to move on; now, that's important."

"What do you mean?"

"You seem to be afraid that you'll mess up again, and you've put all that weight on your shoulders." Mother Brown inserted.

"Well, isn't that natural? I don't want to disappoint God—"

"You can't disappoint God!" Mother Brown shook her head. "Choice, He knows all and sees all. He knew you before you were ever formed in your mother's womb, and He knew every sin you would commit before you were ever born."

"I know that, but now that Jesus has saved me, I don't want to fall back—"

"I understand that, Choice, and I commend you for your commitment to your faith." Mother Brown nodded her agreement. "But Jesus doesn't want us to serve Him in fear of what *might* happen."

"But if I'm not careful, I could go back to my old life, or worse."

"Choice, we're saved by God's grace, but it doesn't stop there." Mother Brown intreated. "He helps us to grow in grace, too. Christ died and rose again so we can be free from fear in this life…even the fear of sin. He wants us to know that His blood keeps on cleansing, and that's what keeps us saved…not our own works."

"But how can I be sure I won't do anything wrong again?" Choice countered.

"Is that why you're so hard on yourself and judge others so harshly, because you're afraid you might sin again?" Mother Brown softened.

Choice thought for a moment. "Yeah, I guess so."

"Choice, you *will* sin again." Mother Brown answered. "We sin every day…in that thing we do, or say, or think that's not like God. But we have to believe His grace is sufficient to cover all our sins. We have to trust Jesus…not ourselves."

"But don't I have to strive to be good?" Choice rebutted.

"Good luck with that one." Mother Brown grinned. "Girl, you couldn't *strive* to make yourself good before you accepted Jesus; what makes you think you can do it now?" she said soberly. "What you must do is trust that Jesus has already made you *good* by exchanging your sin for His righteousness."

"But don't I have to try to do right?" Choice sagged.

"Yes, out of love for Jesus; not out of fear of sin. Love is freedom. Fear is bondage."

Choice shook her head. "I don't get it."

"You're not going to go out and try to sin because you love Jesus." Mother Brown agreed. "But He knows we're not going to behave perfectly as long as we're in these bodies, so He made provision for us through His grace.

His provision of grace allows us to grow from our mistakes and continue to live on—"

"But—"

"Choice, your drugs were no worse than my overeating." Mother Brown popped the last of her second slice of bread into her mouth.

"How can you say that?" Choice scowled.

"Okay, maybe it's not criminal, but it's just as visible. If I eat one cookie, only I know; but if I eat ten cookies, everybody knows." Mother Brown snickered.

Choice listened.

"But as with any other sin, I have to ask the Lord to forgive me, believe that He's forgiven me, and move on." Mother Brown insisted. "If I sit around obsessing over the ten cookies I ate last night, I'll end up eating twenty today! That's the nature of sin."

"Oh, I see."

"We have a tendency to do what we *don't* want to do, and that's why God gives us grace." Mother Brown continued. "He has forgiven you, Choice. Now, you've got to trust Him, forgive yourself, and move on. You see, my dear, sweet Choice, the fear of sin is as much bondage as the sin itself. Jesus knows this. That's why He died for *all* our sins…past, present and future…so we can be free to live and grow in His amazing grace."

"But how can I be sure of that?" Choice retorted.

"Choice, you've got to get out of your own head and take Jesus at His word: 'It…is…finished!'"

"Oh, I've been so wrong." Choice reeled like a heavy load was being lifted off her shoulders. "Jesus *really* does love me!"

"Yes, He does, Choice." Mother Brown assured her. "He paid your price in full. He saved you by His grace, and now it's time to lighten up and let Him grow you...by His grace.

Choice broke down and wept, like a dam of pent-up emotions had burst inside her.

Iris climbed down from her booster chair and into Choice's lap. "No cry," she said tenderly; and ever so gently, she wiped away every one of Choice's tears with her sweet, little fingers.

# CHAPTER 25: MINISTER TO ONE ANOTHER.

*I Peter 4:10*

The Texas sun was agreeably bright and beautiful on the second Sunday in May, 2008. It was Mother's Day morning, and the congregation streamed into Overcoming Faith looking like a pastel parade. Everyone was decked out in their best spring frock, topped off with a red or white carnation to honor and pay tribute to their mother. The red flowers signified a living mother; the white represented a mother who had gone home to be with the Lord.

Before the worship service began, Sensay corralled Choice in the lobby and steered her into his office. She was dressed in a lovely coral maxi with a white carnation pinned over her heart. Sensay was dressed in his finest white robe trimmed in burgundy silk.

"You're looking mighty pretty," Sensay said as he led Choice to a seat at his desk. "You haven't been avoiding me; have you?"

"No," Choice mumbled, "I've just been doing a lot of soul searching; that's all."

"Oh, yeah." Sensay smiled. "Anything I can do to help?"

"You already have," Choice said, straining to keep her tears in check.

"How so?"

"You told me I had to forgive my mom and aunt...Marian." Choice sniffed. "And you were right. Mother Brown was right. The Bible is right. There's no way I can move forward if I hang out in my past."

"Amen." Sensay reached for her hand. The very touch of it made his heart dance. "Because I really want you to move forward, Choice...with me."

Choice drew in her breath. "Do you mean that, Sensay?"

"Yes, with all my heart. I've even told the Pastor about us—"

"Us?"

"Well, at least my half of *us*, and he's ready to talk to us anytime—"

"Don't you think that's a little premature?"

"Not from where I sit." Sensay firmed. "I know I don't know everything there is to know about you, Choice. And you don't know everything about me. But I do know two important things—"

"What's that?"

"You love the Lord, and I love you."

Choice's heart pranced like a baby doe. "How do you know I love the Lord?"

"Because you do what He says...even when you're not feeling it." Sensay held both of her hands in his. "Look at you now. You're willing to forgive Marian, even though she hurt you, very deeply." He squeezed her hands. "And

I want to walk with you through this, Choice. I want to walk with you through the rest of your life."

"Sensay, I've never heard anything so sweet." Choice shivered. "But I don't know if I love you—"

"Do you respect me?"

"Of course, I do. You're a wonderful, compassionate man of God—"

"Then we'll start there and build on it." Sensay gently caressed her cheek. "What do you say?"

"I say, yes." Choice's auburn eyes beamed. "I'm willing to try."

Sensay wanted to pull her into his arms and kiss her until his love was enough for the two of them, but he was due in the pulpit and with Evangelist Mayberry home ill, his service was needed. Instead, he lifted Choice up from her chair and encircled her in his loving arms. "I hate to rush us like this, Baby," he whispered, "but it's pulpit time."

Sensay's body heat sent chills clear down to Choice's core. Her knees went weak, but she managed to pull herself away. "I understand," she whispered.

"We'll finish…we'll start this conversation again later; okay?"

"Go." Choice's nostrils swelled with pride. "You don't want to be late for a very important date."

"I love you," Sensay mouthed as he walked out of the door.

Finally, alone, Choice sank back into the chair and let her happy tears flow.

\*\*\*\*

It was obvious that Pastor Mayberry's heart was heavy as he mounted the pulpit, despite the standing-room-only Mother's Day crowd. The ushers had resorted to placing folding chairs along the aisles to accommodate the numbers. Traditionally, this was the Sunday that even non-believers flocked to church, and pastors were expected to come forth with a swelling evangelistic message to win souls, but Pastor Mayberry was having none of it. He needed to set the flock straight.

Evangelist Mayberry was visibly absent, and it didn't take long before the regulars were putting their collective heads together as to why. Assistant Pastor Sensay had been left to handle the call to worship alone, with his eyes squarely planted on Choice, in advance of Pastor Mayberry taking the podium.

"Saints and friends," Pastor Mayberry began. "It's at times like these we need to pray."

"Amen."

"I would ask you to pray for your First Lady this morning because she's been in bed with a migraine headache for three whole days." Pastor Mayberry confided. "She's resting comfortably, but some of you know what that's like."

"Amen."

"It seems just when the hand of the Lord starts moving on your behalf, the enemy tries to steal your joy."

"All right, Pastor!"

"And the wicked one will use anybody," the pastor boomed, wiping his brow, "your worst enemy, or your closest friend. But it's at times like these that we have to hold on...hold onto our faith, Church!" he bellowed. "Because the more we see what human nature is capable of, the more we ought to worship our Lord. You ask me, why? 'Cause there ain't nobody like Jesus; that's why!"

"Hallelujah!"

Pastor Mayberry locked his eyes over in the Deacon's corner, making note of the missing Deacon Bliss. "Every man, woman, boy or girl on this planet wants to have his or her own way," he continued. "We've got men who've taken vows, plotting to leave their wives. We've got old men trying to have their way with young girls. It's man's nature to sin!"

Pastor Mayberry looked back at the congregation. "But only Jesus was willing to give up His rights for us...come down and pay for all our sins...so we can live and not die...so we can have the right to eternal life. Jesus gave us love in exchange for our mess. Jesus is a true friend, Church! He's the only one we've got, and His way is right!"

"Yes, sir, Preacher!"

"Who else has might and mercy…at the same time?" The pastor paused for effect. "Think about it. Everybody we know who's mighty…who has great power…has very little mercy. Think of Hitler, Nero, Idi Amin and all the rest. And everyone we know who's merciful…who's kind beyond measure…is considered weak and powerless. But not Jesus! Jesus had the mercy to give his life away for your sins and mine on Calvary's cross; and then he had the awesome power to take up His life again and get up from the grave on that third day morning. Who else could do that? Who else would do that…for you and for me?"

"Nobody!"

"Stand to your feet and let's sing out this morning, Church, "Praise God for His marvelous mercies!"

As the congregation began to sing from the depths of its soul, Tyrone got up from the very back pew where he'd been camped out like a stowaway. He made his way to find Rachael who was sitting with Jake near the front.

"Tyrone?" Rachael's mouth dropped when she saw him standing there. "What're you doing here?"

Jake's eyes lit up.

Tyrone squeezed in on her row. "Do you trust me?" he asked Rachael.

"Yes." Rachael responded to the determination in his eyes—the strength of character that had drawn her to him when they'd first met.

"Do you trust me enough to spend the rest of your life with me…and Jake?"

"Yes."

Tyrone took his little family, one in each hand, and led them to the altar. He had no clue it wasn't the appropriate time, but Pastor Mayberry honored his coming. He came down from the pulpit and formed a circle with Tyrone and his family, and they prayed.

"Pastor," Tyrone said, "I was baptized as a baby, but I want to be baptized again because today I finally understood who Jesus is…for myself."

"Fine, son."

"And Pastor," Tyrone pressed. "This is my family, Rachael and Jake." He turned to Rachael. "And if she'll have me, my wife and son."

"Yes," was all Rachael could manage. Her eyes rimmed with burning tears and her heart was threatening to explode. This is all she'd ever wanted—to make a family with Tyrone.

Assistant Pastor Sensay came down from the pulpit, and they prayed again while the congregation sang; and they kept singing, and singing like they would never stop.

# CHAPTER 26: DEFRAUD NOT
# ONE ANOTHER.

*I Thessalonians 4:6*

Bright and early Monday morning, however, was quite a different story. There was singing all right, but it was not of an angelic nature. It was Miss Wanda Lewis from the church's audit firm, Massey & Massey, singing her song of woe.

"I can't have my Finance Director going off half-cocked," was what Pastor Mayberry had said to her when he ordered her to perform a secret, emergency audit of the church's finances. He had made the request the previous Thursday, immediately after Mother Brown told him the story Rachael had learned from Deacon Bliss. Rachael had told Mother Brown about Bliss being her daddy and his plans to divorce his wife, Marvella. Now, it was Miss Lewis' turn to tell her tale.

"For the most part, Pastor Mayberry," the prim middle-aged woman reported, "the church's finances are in excellent shape. I was happy to discover that the church has been making great strides toward reaching its $6 million goal in order to build the new Children's Education Building for cash. You're over halfway there. There's more than $3 million in the account."

"Yes-yes." Pastor Mayberry rushed her along. He hated getting up this early on Mondays. "Is that all?"

"No, that's not all." Miss Lewis pushed her readers up on her nose. "I'm very sorry to report that I did find some irregularities with the account—"

"Which account?"

"The Annex Fund account, of course."

Pastor Mayberry bolted upright. "What kind of irregularities?"

"Your church's bylaws call for there to be at least two signatures on every account."

"Yes-yes."

"And your name, along with Assistant Pastor Sensay Logan and Deacon Bliss, appears as signatory to every major account…with the exception of one."

"Which one?" Pastor Mayberry spurted.

"The Annex Fund."

"The *Annex Fund*! That's our largest account."

"Correct." Miss Lewis agreed. "But your name does not appear on it. If you will recall I cautioned you in last year's audit report that you should not allow each account to have separate signatories. If you will recall my recommendation was that all of the accounts require three signatures, with you being one of the signatories on every account."

"Okay. But whose name does appear?" Pastor Mayberry quizzed.

"Appear on what?"

"On our biggest account…the *Annex Fund*!"

"That would be." Miss Lewis flipped the pages. "Deacon Raython Bliss and Evangelist Johnesther Mayberry. That's your wife isn't it?"

"Yes." Pastor Mayberry sank into his chair. He felt like a drowning man. "My name's not there?"

"No," the auditor said curtly. "You didn't know?"

"No. I didn't know." Pastor Mayberry parroted.

"That can't be good."

"No." The pastor felt like he was going down for the third time. "It's not good."

"What course of action would you like me to take?" Miss Lewis readied her pen for action.

Pastor Mayberry gasped for air. "How much is in the Building Fund Account?" He wheezed.

"I understand that account is only used to make minor repairs to the church and other facilities—"

"I know what the account is used for, Miss Lewis." The pastor curbed his irritation; no need to kill the messenger. "What I want to know is how much money is in it?"

Miss Lewis pointed to the bottom line. "As you can see here...$18, 476.28."

"Less than $20,000?"

"Yes."

"What names are on that account?"

"Yours, Sensay Logan's, and Deacon Bliss'."

The pastor spoke with decisive precision. "Then I need you to do *two* very important things for me...today!"

"Yes, sir." Miss Lewis sat at attention. "You just name it."

****

Pastor Mayberry arrived home, haggard and defeated on Monday night, only to find Johnesther still in bed. He pulled up a chair to her bedside.

"Johnesther," the pastor said quietly, "I'm very sorry you've been feeling bad."

"Oh, I'm feeling a little better today." Johnesther granted.

"Good, because there's really something I need to tell you—"

"There's something I need to tell you, too, Mayberry." Johnesther's tone sharpened.

"This is good news, Johnesther." Her husband reloaded. "I've been trying to tell you this since last week, but we've been like ships passing in the night. You see, I had a meeting with—"

"Save it, Mayberry!" Johnesther shut him down. "Whatever you have to say doesn't mean a thing to me anymore."

"Johnesther? What's wrong?"

"Absolutely nothing is wrong. In fact, everything is just right." Evangelist Mayberry popped up in bed like a Jack-in-the-Box. "I've been waiting for years to tell you this."

"To tell me what?"

Johnesther's eyes glazed over with glee. "I'm outta here!" She double-pumped her fist.

"Out of where?"

"Out of your house. Out of your bed. Out of your stupid, little church." Johnesther fumed. "I want a divorce!"

"A divorce?" His wife's announcement hit him like half-a-brick. He'd been playing a lot of scenarios through his head since he found out about the Annex Fund, but never this one.

"You hear me! I can't wait to get out of here—"

"But Johnesther, what about our covenant, our vows?" Pastor Mayberry pleaded. "You're a Minister of the Gospel. How can you—"

"It's because I'm a Minister of the Gospel that I'm leaving you." Johnesther protested. "If I stay here under your thumb, I'll never fulfill my God-given calling. I'll never pastor. I'll never have my own church!"

"But Johnesther, please listen to what I'm trying to tell you—"

"Tell me? I don't want to hear another thing out of your mouth!" The evangelist raged. "I brought the idea of the two services to you. You pooh-poohed that idea. I brought the idea of the satellite church—"

"That was your idea?" Pastor Mayberry gaped. "I thought it came from Bliss—"

"And you poured cold water on that. Don't you get it? I could have been the pastor of the satellite church!" Johnesther bounded out of the bed like a paralytic after a miraculous healing. "But you'll not get another chance to squash my dreams. I *will* have a megachurch!"

"But if the church acts like the world, where will the world go to be saved?"

"What?" Johnesther stomped her bare feet on the carpet. "That's probably why you only have 200 members, Mayberry. Nobody ever has a clue what you're saying."

"But what about Overcoming Faith, Johnesther? You'd tear up the church just to have your own way?"

"You don't get it; do you Mayberry?" Johnesther flung her arms wildly. "You can't tear up a church with less than 200 members. You can only lay it mercifully to rest!"

"But Johnesther, you're my wife—"

"Not anymore I'm not."

"Is there someone else?" Pastor Mayberry tensed.

"Do you think I need another *man* to want to be rid of you, Mayberry? Ha!" Johnesther stared him down. "The divorce papers have been filed, and I'll be out of this dreary hole no later than tomorrow morning." She screamed at him like he wasn't standing there. "Do you hear me, Mayberry? Do you hear me? I'm gone!"

"Please, Johnesther. Listen to me—"

"Mayberry, don't beg. It should be beneath you!" Evangelist Mayberry raced out of the room and slammed the door on their bedroom for the last time.

# CHAPTER 27: GREET ONE ANOTHER WITH A HOLY KISS.

*II Corinthians 13:12*

Early Tuesday morning, the house phone rang as Johnesther was packing the last of her clothes into her luggage. Pastor Mayberry wasn't there to answer it. Apparently, he'd beat her out of the house. Johnesther started not to answer it, too, but she got a kick out of knowing it would be her very last time.

"Hello!" Johnesther managed to catch it before the other party hung up.

"Good morning, my dear sister. Is this Evangelist Mayberry?"

"It is. Who's this?"

"This is your brother from over at New Bethel Outreach. We met some time ago at your husband's Appreciation Service. I'm Deacon Banks. Do you recall?"

"Oh, yes, Deacon Banks," Johnesther said smoothly. "I didn't recognize your voice at first."

"I understand."

"How can I help you?"

Deacon Banks paused, puzzled. "Have you given any thought to our offer?"

"What offer?" Evangelist Mayberry stammered.

"Surely, Pastor Mayberry has told you by now."

"No. I'm sorry." The evangelist equivocated. "I don't know what you mean. This is my first day up in nearly a week. I've been down with a violent migraine."

"Then I understand. I'm sure Pastor Mayberry didn't want to put any heavy decisions on your mind with you in that condition."

"No. I guess not," Johnesther said, gliding into it. "But Deacon Banks, maybe you can enlighten me."

"I hate to steal your husband's thunder—"

"Oh, I'm pretty sure he won't mind. After all, we are both pastors, you know."

"Yes, we do know, and very fine ones at that. Your credentials and your labor precede you."

Johnesther giggled. "What a kind thing to say."

"I say it not only out of kindness, but need," the deacon said bluntly.

"Need? What need?"

"You will recall we lost our pastor—"

"Oh, yes, it was such tragic news…and so sudden."

"Yes, sister, I tell you it hit us rather hard."

"I can only imagine—"

"But we're moving on; it's all we can do."

"Of course—"

"And that's why we asked Pastor Mayberry to share our…offer…with you last week."

Johnesther pushed him along. "Yes, I think Mayberry did mention that he'd a very productive meeting last week—"

"The meeting was with us, and we asked Pastor Mayberry to extend an offer to you."

"An offer?" Johnesther puzzled.

"Yes, for you to pastor our flock," Deacon Banks said plainly. "We're small, but we're coming, and our outreach efforts—"

"Did you say...pastor...me?" Johnesther quivered like a shell-shock victim.

"Yes, Evangelist, we would be honored if you would accept. We have great plans to share the mission field with Overcoming Faith—"

"I can't—" Johnesther flopped into a kitchen chair; her mind as green and thick as pea soup.

"Pardon me, sister. I can barely hear you."

"I can't...talk right now...my head...aches."

"Of course, I understand." Deacon Banks accepted. "But please call us back at your earliest convenience. I'm sure you can understand we're really being pressured to make a decision by our leadership. We've been without a pastor—"

Johnesther hung up on the man and escaped into the bathroom just in time to hold her head over the toilet. *Barf!* She was really going to be sick.

**** 

Bliss met Johnesther at the North Dallas Luxury Suites Hotel as soon as she checked in on Tuesday afternoon.

She offered him a seat on her ostrich-colored couch. It was a perfect match to the muted tones that graced the elegant stateroom and the floor-to-ceiling drapes that crowned the view to the balcony. The Spanish-styled balcony was paved in expansive Mexican tile and trimmed in a bronzed wrought iron railing, topped off with menacing ceramic gargoyles.

"The strangest thing happened today, Bliss." Johnesther postured.

"Strange?" Bliss needled. "Do you mean strange like leaving your husband of nearly thirty years?"

"No, not that," Johnesther carped, "something far more meaningful than that!"

"What then?"

"Deacon Banks…from over at New Bethel…called me this morning before I made my final exit from that house and all its gruesome memories."

"For what?"

"To offer me a job." Johnesther disclosed.

"A job? What job?"

"As Pastor of New Bethel Outreach Church."

Bliss hooted. "You gotta be kidding. You sure?"

"Of course, I'm sure." Johnesther bristled. "I know a job offer when I hear one; don't I?"

"But why? Why now?"

"I guess Mayberry's been trying to tell me this for days, but I've been avoiding him. My migraine; remember?"

"Oh, yeah." Bliss caressed her body with his eyes. "But from the looks of it, Sis. Legs, you've made a full recovery."

"Well, I had to tell the man something; didn't I? I didn't want him pawing all over me in my bed or asking me a thousand questions."

"No, I guess not, 'specially since you're giving him the axe and having him foot the bill." The deacon chuckled.

"Bliss!"

"But I wonder why New Bethel would come a-callin' now?"

"They've been without a pastor for some time." Johnesther flamed. "Why wouldn't they make me the offer? I'll make a great pastor."

"True-dat, but—"

"And Deacon Banks also mentioned forming some sort of alliance with Overcoming Faith, but I didn't get it—"

"So, what did you tell the man?" Bliss frowned.

"Nothing."

"Nothing?"

"I couldn't finish the conversation." Johnesther squirmed. "It took me too much by surprise, especially today when I was packing to leave Mayberry."

"Yeah, that could be a little awkward." Bliss smirked. "So, what're you going to do?"

"Nothing."

"Nothing?"

"I can't take that job, not now; not when they hear I'm divorcing Mayberry." Johnesther reasoned. "Besides, I don't know if I would even want to pastor that church."

"Why not?"

"New Bethel? It's just one step up from a storefront; and who would ever want to pastor a storefront church?" Evangelist Mayberry giggled. "The congregation is as small as Overcoming Faith, and there's no real growth potential."

"But I hear they have a terrific outreach program."

"Sure, if you want to deal with hoodlums, prostitutes and at-risk teens—"

"Yeah, I bet there's lots o' baby-mamma drama over there…oo-wee!" Bliss grinned. "Them the kind o' folk that's too sorry to pick up the paper from 'round their own feet."

"That's what I'm saying." Johnesther agreed. "I don't want to deal with those kinds of people or their headaches anymore…talking about migraines. It's like pulling teeth trying to keep them from becoming dropouts, or whores, or thugs, or worse."

"That's right!"

"And half these people just want a handout—"

"You got that right!" Bliss pumped her up. "They can hear a wallet opening from a mile off and come running to see how they can get over on ya."

"Well stated." Johnesther preened. "These people aren't looking to do better; they just want something for nothing."

"I think you're right." Bliss agreed. "New Bethel would be the same song, different verse. And let's face it; you've burned all your bridges on the Southside of town."

"Good riddance to bad rubbish; that's what I say." Johnesther crossed her legs and let her sweeping red satin robe slide up one knee. "I want to be here in North Dallas where the people are teachable, eager to learn, and loyal to their pastor—"

"Not to mention…rich."

"Well, you can't grow a megachurch without tithes and offerings." Johnesther snapped her bejeweled fingers. "Oh, speaking of money, Bliss, let's go down to the bank and transfer the Annex Fund to our account, right now."

"No, Johnesther, we'll go on Thursday morning."

"But why?" Johnesther pouted.

"It's getting too late in the banking day to go rushing over there. We don't want to look hurried or suspicious; do we?" Bliss wrung his hands like a chintzy miser. "No, ma'am. When we go strutting in there to pick up our millions, we want to look cool, calm and collected."

"So why can't we go tomorrow?" Johnesther whined.

"I've got to go to Tyler tomorrow on some company business. I'll be back by Thursday. We'll go then; promise." Deacon Bliss moved over to the house phone. "Besides, sounds like you need some TLC."

"I am a little tired."

"Then it's time for us to celebrate!" Bliss picked up the phone and ordered a bottle of champagne.

"Alcohol?" Johnesther sniffed. "You drink alcohol?"

"It's just champagne, Evangelist. It won't hurt a bit."

"I guess, just one glass—"

"Come here, Woman." Bliss signaled her to come and sit on his lap.

"Stop it, Bliss. It's not time for that yet."

"Then come over here and let me rub on them fine legs so a brother can at least get a preview of coming attractions." Bliss drooled. "I've been waiting in line a long time for you, Baby."

Johnesther sauntered across the room, robe trailing like a movie star. She sat on his lap. "Bliss! Ohhh! Bliss!"

# CHAPTER 28: GRUDGE NOT AGAINST ONE ANOTHER.

*James 5:9*

It was the long-awaited night for the members of W.O.O.F. to celebrate. It had been exactly one year since they'd assembled to buy into Mother Brown's vision of "keeping the *wolf* at the door through service and celibacy." The decorating committee, which consisted of Choice and Rachael, had done a bang-up job with their little meeting room. It was strung with yellow butterflies throughout to symbolize their newfound freedom and Mother Brown's favorite color.

As everyone straggled into the W.O.O.F meeting, Laqueeta pulled them all together before Mother Brown arrived.

"Y'all! Y'all!" Laqueeta quacked. "Sit down. Sit down. You gotta hear this!" They each took a seat in a tight, little circle. "I heard that Deacon Bliss *and* Evangelist Mayberry have filed for divorce."

"Divorce?" Fancy hopped up, cheeks ablaze. "She can't do that! She didn't tell me!"

"Sit down, Girl!" Laqueeta snapped. "Why in the world would she tell *you* of all people? She don't even know you're alive."

"Yeah, Fancy." Rachael puzzled. "Why would she tell you?"

"Shut your face, Rachael!" Fancy yelled so hard the blast kicked her back into her chair.

"Is something going on between Johnesther and Bliss?"

"Who knows?"

"I guess anything's possible."

"I hear Johnesther got crosswise with Pastor 'cause he wouldn't let her have a satellite church up in North Dallas," Laqueeta said.

Choice chimed in, "Well, according to Sensay—"

"Oh, so it's Sensay now; is it?" Laqueeta needled.

Choice ignored her. "Sensay said Pastor doesn't want to take on any new projects until we finish the Children's Education Building."

"So maybe she's just going to North Dallas with Deacon Bliss to start a new church of her own?" Gabbi's eyes flashed. "But I totally don't know—"

"I don't care how you try to dress up this pig," Laqueeta quipped, "there ain't no high-class way to do a low-down thing."

"And you should know," Choice retorted.

"Look, Trick—"

"I never thought something like this could happen at Overcoming Faith." Angel flapped. She had trusted in her church, and her faith was starting to crumble.

"I guess Pastor is a broken man," Rachael said.

"Maybe not." Choice glared at Laqueeta, daring her to interrupt. "Sensay said Pastor had some good news, too.

New Bethel, around the corner, wants to partner with us on the Children's Education Building—"

"How so?"

"I don't know the details, but they have a big outreach program, and they want to use our new facility and share in the costs."

"Well, that only makes sense." Rachael agreed. "It's about time all these churches on every corner stop building all these high-priced structures and start building up these broken-down kids."

"Amen!"

"But for the grace of God—"

"Who cares about all that?" Fancy's hands shook uncontrollably. Her face was blowing up like a balloon about ready to explode. "None of that matters!"

"I don't understand." Rachael glared at the sweat popping off her forehead. "Why are you so bent out o' shape about this? You don't have no skin in the game—"

"Shut your face, Rachael Jones!" Fancy lunged at her. "You and your lil' brat oughta go back to sleeping in your car where you belong!"

"Say what *#$%*?!? Rachael shrilled, taking a flying leap in her direction. The others quickly laid hands on her while Fancy staggered blindly out of the room, nearly bowling over Mother Brown in the doorway.

"What's going on in here?" Mother Brown recovered. "What's wrong with Fancy?"

"Crazy!" Laqueeta said with a crack of her gum. "Ain't y'all noticed?"

****

Out in the hallway, Fancy flashed open her cell phone and hit up Evangelist Mayberry on speed dial. The right side of her face was twitching, and her right eye was blinking like a bad light bulb.

"What's this I hear about you getting a divorce?" Fancy sizzled as soon as Johnesther answered.

"Who is this?" Johnesther flared. The voice on the other end was unrecognizable.

"It's Fancy!" she slurred; her tongue was beginning to swell. "You *can-not* get a divorce!"

"First of all," Johnesther blasted, "I don't know who you think you are, calling me like this! And second of all, I don't answer to you!"

"Do you know how much time and money I've spent?" Fancy's whole body was shaking like a paint mixer. "I doubled my hours. I worked two jobs. I took out loans; all to become the lead attorney for Overcoming Faith!" She wailed like a she-wolf caught in a trap. "I've worked. I've slaved. I've killed myself to pass the bar; all to head-up the legal team for the new Children's wing. I...I trusted you, Johnesther!"

"Who asked you to?" Johnesther's words were as cold as frozen icicles and twice as deadly. "Don't you *ever* call me again. You...you...second-generation lunatic!" She clicked off the line.

"Johnesther! Johnesther Mayberry!" Fancy screamed into the dead connection. She ran howling and clawing down the sides of the hallway like a mad woman. Her feet and arms were groping wildly, like they were attached to the wrong body. The ungodly commotion caused people to bail out of their meeting rooms to see what was happening.

Fancy flew out of the church's front door like a tormented twister, staggering blindly into the busy parking lot. Despite the blaring horns and screeching tires, Fancy pitched herself in front of an oncoming car. The driver swerved to miss her, but he clipped her under his wheels. The W.O.O.F. members reached the parking lot just in time to see Fancy, mangled and lying in a pool of her own blood.

Rachael dialed 911. Angel tried to calm Gabbi who was screaming at the top of her lungs. Mother Brown was wringing her hands and saying, "I should've known poor Fancy was under too much pressure."

Choice and Laqueeta called a truce long enough to help Mother Brown into Rachael's car. Afterwards, they all piled in and followed the ambulance to a nearby hospital.

In the still, coldness of the waiting room, they all joined hands in solidarity for their fallen sister. Choice held Laqueeta's hand, and Rachael led them in prayer.

# CHAPTER 29: DO NOT BITE AND DEVOUR ONE ANOTHER.

*Galatians 5:15*

When Johnesther Mayberry strutted into The First National Bank on the arm of Deacon Raython Bliss that beautiful Thursday morning in May, the room paused. She was stunning in a royal blue St. John knit with a matching hat of royal blue peacock feathers swirled around the crown. Her shoes were royal blue stilettos with skinny gold heels. Her jewelry was the finest Chanel had to offer—18 carat yellow gold and canary diamonds. Bliss dipped one broad shoulder and *dap-walked* in, decked out from head to toe in a navy pin-striped suit with a gold tie and hankie to match. His feet were donned in the world's finest navy ostrich boots.

They didn't sit. They stood in the waiting area until one of the representatives came over to greet them.

"Good morning," she said. "I'm Ms. Blankingship. May I help you?"

"You most certainly can, Little Miss." Bliss smiled broadly. "We're here to transact a little church business."

"Then step over to my desk, please," the rep said. "I'll be happy to assist you."

Bliss was bubbling, and Johnesther allowed him to take the lead. "We're from Overcoming Faith Church, and we need to close out an account," he said with a glossy smile.

"Do you have the account number?"

"Why, certainly Little Lady, why else would we be here?" Bliss pushed the church's account card toward her. "Give us the account with *our* names on it."

"Yes, sir. I can pull up that account." The bank rep looked at Bliss incredulously. "What are your names?"

"Oh, I'm sorry, Little Lady. I'm Deacon Raython Bliss, Finance Director, and this here is Evangelist Johnesther Mayberry, the Pastor's wife."

"Our manager likes to meet with our customers," Ms. Blankingship said politely, "when they're closing an account of this magnitude."

"Well, send him right over." Bliss checked his gold Rolex timepiece. "But we're running on a tight timetable, so make it snappy."

"Yes, sir. I'll get him right away."

After a few moments, Ms. Blankingship emerged with a skinny little man at her heels. "This is our manager, Mr. Langston," she said.

"Good morning, Mr. Bliss and Mrs. Mayberry." Mr. Langston smiled dolefully, taking a seat behind the desk. "When any of our clients close a substantial account, we always like to ask if there's anything we can do to retain their business. Are there any other services—"

"Hold on, right there," Bliss carped. "There is absolutely nothing wrong with yo' service, and the church has been immensely pleased with yo' bank."

"Then why're you closing this account today, sir?"

Bliss and Johnesther squirmed a little. "Like I said," Bliss continued, "we're pleased with yo' service, but an investment opportunity has landed on our doorstep, and we'd like to take full advantage of it."

"Of course, I understand," the bank manager agreed. "I just wanted to be sure that your decision today was not prompted by any lack of attention on our part—"

"Oh, no!" Johnesther couldn't resist getting involved. "Not in the least."

"Very well, then." The bank manager gave them a stiff smile. "How do you want to handle this transaction? Do you want us to wire the funds to another account; a cashier's check—"

"We'll take a cashier's check." Johnesther smiled lustfully.

"Very well, I'll bring Ms. Blankenship back over to complete the transaction." Mr. Langston rose and gave Bliss a firm handshake. "It's a pleasure meeting you and doing business with you." He looked from Bliss to Johnesther. "If there's anything we can do for you in the future, please don't hesitate to call on us. Good day."

Johnesther's heart quit pounding in her ears. "That wasn't bad, Bliss," she whispered.

"I told you if we came in here relaxed and in charge, we would have no worries. Didn't I tell you that?"

"Yes, Bliss." Johnesther stroked his ego. "That's exactly what you said."

Ms. Blankingship reappeared with the appropriate papers. She sat at her desk and slid them over to the duo. "Each of you needs to sign here and here." She pointed to where 'x' marked the spot.

"Sure thing, Little Lady." Bliss signed first and then passed the papers and pen over to Johnesther.

"All right," Ms. Blankingship said. "Wait right here, and I'll go over to the teller window and pick up your cashier's check."

Bliss buzzed as soon as they were alone. "This $3-plus million will be just enough to get us going, Johnesther," he said, showing off. "I've done the math."

"What do you mean?"

"Well, as you well know, real estate prices in North Dallas are as high as a Georgia pine." Bliss puffed. "It's going to take this amount just to get us into a church, and then it'll take more to get us up and running."

"That's no problem, Bliss." Johnesther went along with his boasting. "Once we get into a church, we can make upgrades as we see fit over time."

"True. True. I guess you're right." Bliss nodded. "The main thing is to use this $3-plus million to buy a church we like, in a good location, and start from there."

"It won't take long for us to attract the kind of clientele…parishioners that will put us over the top."

"That's your department, Johnesther—"

"And you'd better believe I'll handle it." Evangelist Mayberry sneered.

"All right, Sis. Legs, I believe you." Bliss licked his lips. "Shush up, now. We're on the home stretch. Here comes that woman with our check."

Ms. Blankingship floated back into her seat. "Well, here we have it," she announced, "your cashier's check." She pushed it across the desk to Bliss, and Johnesther intercepted it. "Is there anything else I can do for you this morning?"

Johnesther opened the check. Her mouth moved, but no words came out.

Bliss patted her hand. "What's wrong, Johnesther?"

She dropped the check, and Bliss caught it before it hit the floor. "What's the meaning of this?" he bellowed.

"Sir, I don't understand." Ms. Blankenship blinked.

Johnesther was gasping for air.

Bliss was pointing at the amount. "This cashier's check is for $18,476.28," he roared. "That's less than $20,000."

"Yes, sir. Exactly."

Sweat was beading off Johnesther's forehead like popping corn. She was waving her hand-fan, double-time, trying to find some relief.

"What are you trying to pull here?" Bliss persisted. "This check is from the Building Fund account!"

"Yes, sir."

Johnesther's feet slid from under her chair. Her skirt rolled up one prized thigh.

Bliss shot a glance at Johnesther's failing form, but carried on with his tirade. "Look, Lady, I told you to give us the funds from the account with *our* names on it…me and Johnesther, here." Deacon Bliss jabbed a finger in her direction. "The *Annex Fund!* We're supposed to be picking up over $3 million!"

"I'm sorry, sir, but the only account that has your names on it *is* the Building Fund." Ms. Blankingship corrected.

Bliss jumped up, squeezing the short-changed check in his greedy palm. "This can't be right!" He stormed. "I demand to see the manager!"

Ms. Blankingship stiffened. "It is exactly right, sir. The signatories on the Annex Fund are…Deacon Black, Trustee Jarvis, and…Pastor Mayberry," she read. "There's no way you can get your hands on that money."

Bliss whooped around in his fine ostrich boots, swinging the bogus check overhead. He put on such a war dance atop Ms. Blankingship's desk, the other customers and tellers went running for cover.

Security placed a call—The Dallas Police Department.

About that time, Johnesther's eyes rolled to the top of her head; she turned a violent shade of blue, which clashed horribly with her impeccable outfit, and she crashed to the floor with a loud thud. Her stilettos went one way and her peacock-feathered hat the other. Her $1,000 skirt rolled so far up her assets; Ms. Blankingship had to peel off her bargain-basement jacket to cover up her nakedness.

Security placed a second call—911.

# EPILOGUE

## Prophetess Johnesther Mayberry and
## Elder Raython Bliss
## Overcoming Faith Prophetic Ministries
## Far North Dallas

Given the price of real estate in North Dallas, the check for less than $20,000 skimmed from the Building Fund account could only lease a store front on Alpha Road, near I-635. Of course, a storefront church was *not* what Johnesther had in mind, but with her new title and Bliss at her side, she's beginning to attract her kind of people.

Prophetess Mayberry dons the pulpit each Sunday in some stunning variation of her gold crown hat and purple robe, playing the Queen Esther role to the hilt. Invariably, she's ushered to the platform by Elder Raython Bliss, decked out in all black, from his ten-gallon hat to his alligator boots.

The growing congregation is a rainbow of rich, aggressive, mostly female members. They are of the restless, itching-ear variety, always looking for some new and different spin on God's word. And Johnesther never disappoints. She can make chicken feathers sound like chicken soup, and her rhetoric is sufficiently vague to allow her flock to keep right on living their own sorted lifestyles.

In addition to servicing Johnesther since before the ink dried on their two-headed divorce, Bliss is also taking full advantage of being nearly the only rooster in the gilded hen house. Behind Johnesther's back, he's making many a late-night visit to ease the troubled minds of the female flock.

As predicted, the offering plates are overflowing. If Bliss can manage to keep all of his chickens in the coop, he estimates, "We'll be riding high in a multi-million-dollar church before the year's out!"

By the way, Marvella saw no reason to contest the divorce. She's lost a *happy* hundred pounds, and she has to beat the men off with a stick. *Go, Girl!*

# PASTOR JOHN MAYBERRY
## OVERCOMING FAITH CHURCH

When asked why he allowed Bliss and Johnesther to run off with the church's Building Fund account, Pastor Mayberry explained, "I wanted to fix it so those two could never double back to Overcoming Faith, even if I have to pay the money back myself." He did so, happily, and made no effort to contest the divorce.

As soon as the agreement was struck with New Bethel Outreach, construction plans got underway on the new Children's Education Building in June, 2008. New Bethel is keeping up its end of the bargain, and they've also hired a new pastor, Lucinda Boyd. Pastor Boyd has a long resume of caring concern for at-risk youth, and she is strengthening the fellowship and the outreach between the two churches. It's as Bro. Davis predicted, "We gotta work with one another to help these damaged kids."

Thanks to the combined outreach efforts, the congregation at Overcoming Faith has doubled. Young converts are flocking to the church. The nose rings, dreds, and tattoos are beginning to outnumber the hat-wearing crowd, but through the help of the Spirit, they're all finding a way to get along.

Pastor Lucinda Boyd, by the way, is beautiful, single and just a few years younger than Pastor Mayberry. She has never capitalized on her many opportunities to marry.

Despite a number of would-be suitors over the years, her work has always come first.

Operating as satellite churches, Pastor Mayberry and Pastor Boyd are putting their heads together on many worthwhile projects. They're drawn to one another by their mutual interests, their similar backgrounds, and their committed love for the Lord. *Hmmmm.*

# LAQUEETA LEE
## EX-W.O.O.F.

Laqueeta quit her good-paying job so she and her two boys could run off to Vegas with her boyfriend, Rodney. Everything was peachy-keen until Rodney lost all her money at the blackjack tables. Afterwards, he started getting high and using Laqueeta for a punching bag. Laqueeta felt she had to stay because she didn't want to go back to Dallas with her tail tucked between her legs.

But when Rodney beat her eldest son, Mack, and made his brother, Mike, watch in horror that was too much, even for Laqueeta. She waited good until Rodney fell fast asleep one night in one of his drunken stupors, and then she and the boys duct taped him to the bed, from head to foot.

It was rumored that it was three days before anybody found Rodney bound and gagged in less than pristine condition. Meanwhile, Laqueeta and her boys rolled him for his wallet and took off in the dead of night. They caught the first thing smoking back to Dallas, which happened to be a Greyhound bus.

Virtually penniless, Laqueeta used her last quarter to call Choice King. Sure, they had had their differences, but Laqueeta knew if she came clean, Choice wouldn't turn her away. She knew in her heart that Choice would treat her like a sister.

Laqueeta smiled through her tears as she dropped her last coin into the payphone at the bus station in downtown Dallas. *Well, Sis. Choice, I guess your prayers for my bad boys got answered after all. And just maybe it is time I traded-up…from sex…to the real love of Christ. I'm just sayin'*

# ANGEL ROJAS
## EX-W.O.O.F.

One Saturday night after a big home win for Denton College, the captain of the football team gave Angel to his offensive line as sort of a *thank you* gift. They boozed it up in a cheap motel room, and then three of the two-hundred-pound linemen held Angel hostage until the next morning, each taking turns against her will. Instead of reporting the multiple rapes to the police, or finding solace in her W.O.O.F. sisters, Angel kept the incident hush-hush. From that time on, however, her life took on a decidedly downward spiral.

The last semester of her senior year, Angel ran off with a pimply-faced blonde, a red-shirt freshman from the men's basketball team. They haven't been seen or heard of since. Angel's distraught parents filed a missing-persons report with the authorities, but there was not much they could do. Angel had just turned twenty-one.

### ALL POINTS BULLETIN (APB)

"Angel Rojas was last seen wearing a black leather cat suit and black studded hip boots. She has a black Mohawk, a skull and cross-bones tattoo on the right side of her neck, and multiple facial piercings. Anybody knowing of her whereabouts is asked to call the Denton Police Department."

# FANCY CHAMBERS
## EX-W.O.O.F.

When Fancy recovered from her extensive injuries after being hit by the car, she was held on a 48-hour suicide watch and psych evaluation in the Psychiatric Ward of Parkview Hospital. She had tried to gouge open her wrists with an un-sterile IV needle.

Fancy was diagnosed as having suffered a complete psychotic break brought on by extreme mental and emotional distress. She broke with reality when her one-sided plot to be rich and famous was abruptly up-ended by Evangelist Johnesther Mayberry who, so unceremoniously, gave her the boot.

Apparently, it had resurfaced Fancy's deep-seated feelings of self-loathing caused by the extreme neglect and abnormal role reversal with her paranoid schizophrenic mother during childhood. After a full 45-day stay in the mental ward, Fancy was released with a fistful of psychotropic meds, which she refused to take, saying, "They make me feel funny."

Anyway, you probably see her every day. She's the bag lady pushing the shopping cart north over the Trinity River Bridge from Oak Cliff into downtown Dallas. You know; the one with the shaggy blonde wig and the bright red lipstick smeared across her face.

At night, Fancy makes her home in a bombed-out Porsche under the bridge. Déjà-vu. During the day, her shopping cart is loaded with black trash bags in the front and a floppy-eared dog with a rhinestone collar in the back. If she'd let you get close enough to overhear her jabbering, you'd learn a thing or two. For one, her dog's name is Johnesther.

# GABRIELLA (GABBI) PRENTISS
# OVERCOMING FAITH CHURCH

The second semester of her senior year at Denton College, a polished announcement appeared, alongside the blonde-haired, straight-toothed smiles of a beautiful, young, well-suited couple, on the front page of Society News in the Dallas Times Herald:

"Miss Gabriella Prudence Prentiss and Mr. Kent Roy Kensington II announced their engagement at a black-tie supper at the Top of the Tower Club last Friday evening. Miss Prentiss is the daughter of Mr. and Mrs. Mark Prentiss of Prentiss & Mason, a prestigious law firm in Fort Worth that specializes in oil and cattle leases. As you know, Mr. Kensington II is the only son of Senator Kent Kensington, the illustrious three-term U.S. Senator from Texas.

Miss Prentiss will graduate with honors from Denton College in May, and Mr. Kensington II is a junior attorney with Kensington & Kensington of Dallas, and an aspiring, young politician in his own right. Will it be long before we see him filling his daddy's big shoes? This reporter thinks not."

****

Gabbi put in a quick call to Rachael as soon as the paper hit the newsstands. "I'm so totally happy, Rach." Gabbi giggled. "It's like this totally awesome miracle! But I couldn't have done it without you, helping me with my studies, or W.O.O.F. praying for me…walking with me." She choked on her happy tears. "And Jesus…He's just like totally rad! *Totally!*"

# TYRONE & RACHAEL JONES-PAIGE AND JAKE
## OVERCOMING FAITH CHURCH

Soon after he proposed at Overcoming Faith, Tyrone took Rachael and Jake to the Justice of the Peace to perform the wedding ceremony. He bought interlocking bands of gold for the occasion, and Mother Brown was the only invited witness. The bride was pretty as the bright summer day they'd chosen in her lavender mini. Her long, thick hair flowed over an airy chiffon collar of white.

Tyrone and Rachael clutched Jake's hand as they pledged their love, and he was beside himself with joy. He and his daddy were dressed in matching black slacks and checkered blazers, and they both wore WWJD buckles on their belts.

One day soon, Tyrone's son is going to have a mighty big name for a little guy—Jake Jones-Paige. His daddy says of the adoption, "I want the *Jones* to remain to honor his mother's never-changing love, and I want the hyphen to forever remind him that no matter how bad things get, they can be changed. Jesus can turn the *paige*!"

## SENSAY & CHOICE KING LOGAN
## OVERCOMING FAITH CHURCH

On a starlit April night in 2009, the new Children's Education Building was dedicated. On bended knee, Sensay presented Choice with a goose-egg-sized diamond engagement ring. Choice was nearly overwhelmed as the throng of well-wishers looked on, but she didn't miss the chance to say, "Yes!" However, she would've been just as satisfied with a cigar band. You see, during the construction process, Choice's feelings had been building for Assistant Pastor Sensay, too, from respect to deep, abiding love. She couldn't wait to begin their new life together, free of her past.

A few months later, they were married on a shiny June morning at Overcoming Faith. Mrs. Rachael Jones-Paige of W.O.O.F. fame served as her Matron of Honor. Mother Brown gave the bride away, and who else but her little granddaughter, Iris, dressed in a long, rosebud satin dress and patent slippers, was the flower girl. Everyone giggled as she came skipping down the gleaming aisle dropping fragrant rose petals along the way. Little Jake Jones-Paige brought up the rear as the ring bearer.

Among the hundreds in attendance, Marian King, an officially invited guest, sat on the Bride's side.

Upon the first chord of the Bridal March, the admiring audience stood in rapt attention. Sensay followed Choice's every step down the aisle. He gave her *that look* a groom in love has for his bride—a mixture of innocence and bliss. He was flanked on both sides by Pastor Mayberry and Pastor Lucinda Boyd who shared in performing the ceremony.

The bride was stunning in white. *Yes!*

## MOTHER BROWN & IRIS BROWN
## PRESIDENT EMERITUS, W.O.O.F.


After seeing her *girls* marry well, Mother Brown decided to retire from the W.O.O.F. ministry. "The Lord helped me get us started; the Bible will do the rest." She would devote her energies full time to her lovely granddaughter, Iris, who'd be starting school soon.

Mother Brown talked Choice King Logan into taking over the W.O.O.F. ministry, and she agreed. "I'll do it if you promise to be close at hand, and if Rachael agrees to work with me."

Mother Brown agreed, ergo her emeritus status. Rachael Jones-Paige agreed, as well. She had heard how Choice helped Laqueeta and her boys get back on their feet; notwithstanding, their hasty retreat back to Dallas, and she was pleased. "Of course, I'll work with Choice," she said. "We're sisters; once a W.O.O.F. member, always a W.O.O.F. member. We love and support one another." However, Rachael will have to fit it into her busy schedule. With Gabbi's encouragement, she's enrolling in night classes at Denton College in the fall.

This year's W.O.O.F class has over 30, eager, young, single women. As much as they will all agree to serve one another and abstain from pre-marital sex, the real drawing card will be finding out how Choice and Rachael got their man. *What? I'm just keeping it real!*

# "ONE-ANOTHER" SCRIPTURES

A Working List of Bible Verses
Compiled by the W.O.O.F. Ministry

### John 13:34
A new commandment I give unto you, That ye love one another; as I have loved you, that ye also love one another.

### John 13:35
By this shall all men know that ye are my disciples, if ye have love one to another.

### Romans 12:5
So we, being many, are one body in Christ, and every one members one of another.

### Romans 12:10
Be kindly affectioned one to another with brotherly love; in honour preferring one another.

### Romans 12:16
Be of the same mind one toward another. Mind not high things, but condescend to men of low estate. Be not wise in your own conceits.

### Romans 13:8
Owe no man anything, but to love one another: for he that loveth another hath fulfilled the law.

## Romans 14:13

Let us not therefore judge one another anymore: but judge this rather, that no man put a stumbling block or an occasion to fall in his brother's way.

## Romans 14:19

Let us therefore follow after the things which make for peace, and things wherewith one may edify another.

## Romans 15:5

Now the God of patience and consolation grant you to be likeminded one toward another according to Christ Jesus.

## Romans 15:7

Wherefore receive ye one another, as Christ also received us to the glory of God.

## Romans 15:14

And I myself also am persuaded of you, my brethren, that ye also are full of goodness, filled with all knowledge, able also to admonish one another.

## Romans 16:16

Salute one another with an holy kiss. The churches of Christ salute you.

## I Corinthians 1:10

Now I beseech you, brethren, by the name of our Lord Jesus Christ, that ye all speak the same thing, and that there be no divisions among you; but that ye be perfectly joined together in the same mind and in the same judgment.

### I Corinthians 4:6

And these things, brethren, I have in a figure transferred to myself and to Apollos for your sakes; that ye might learn in us not to think of men above that which is written, that no one of you be puffed up for one against another.

### I Corinthians 12:25

That there should be no schism in the body; but that the members should have the same care one for another.

### II Corinthians 1:4

Who comforteth us in all our tribulation, that we may be able to comfort them which are in any trouble, by the comfort wherewith we ourselves are comforted of God.

### II Corinthians 13:12

Greet one another with an holy kiss.

### Galatians 5:13

For, brethren, ye have been called unto liberty; only use not liberty for an occasion to the flesh, but by love serve one another.

### Galatians 5:15

But if ye bite and devour one another, take heed that ye be not consumed one of another.

## Galatians 5:26

Let us not be desirous of vain glory, provoking one another, envying one another.

## Galatians 6:2

Bear ye one another's burdens, and so fulfill the law of Christ.

## Ephesians 4:2-3

With all lowliness and meekness, with longsuffering, forbearing one another in love; endeavoring to keep the unity of the Spirit in the bond of peace.

## Ephesians 4:25

Wherefore putting away lying, speak every man truth with his neighbor: for we are members one of another.

## Ephesians 4:32

And be ye kind one to another, tenderhearted, forgiving one another, even as God for Christ's sake hath forgiven you.

## Ephesians 5:21

Submitting yourselves one to another in the fear of God.

## Colossians 3:9

Lie not one to another, seeing that ye have put off the old man with his deeds.

## Colossians 3:13

Forbearing one another, and forgiving one another, if any man have a quarrel against any: even as Christ forgave you, so also do ye.

## Colossians 3:16

Let the word of Christ dwell in you richly in all wisdom; teaching and admonishing one another in psalms and hymns and spiritual songs, singing with grace in your hearts to the Lord.

## 1 Thessalonians 3:12

And the Lord make you to increase and abound in love one toward another, and toward all men, even as we do toward you:

## 1 Thessalonians 4:6

That no man go beyond and defraud his brother in any matter: because that the Lord is the avenger of all such, as we also have forewarned you and testified.

## 1 Thessalonians 4:9

But as touching brotherly love ye need not that I write unto you: for ye yourselves are taught of God to love one another.

## 1 Thessalonians 5:11

Wherefore comfort yourselves together, and edify one another, even as also ye do.

## 1 Timothy 5:21

I charge thee before God, and the Lord Jesus Christ, and the elect angels, that thou observe these things without preferring one before another, doing nothing by partiality.

## Hebrews 3:13

But exhort one another daily, while it is called To day; lest any of you be hardened through the deceitfulness of sin.

## Hebrews 10:24-25

And let us consider one another to provoke unto love and to good works: Not forsaking the assembling of ourselves together, as the manner of some is; but exhorting one another: and so much more, as ye see the day approaching.

## James 4:11

Speak not evil one of another, brethren. He that speaketh evil of his brother, and judgeth his brother, speaketh evil of the law, and judgeth the law: but if thou judge the law, thou art not a doer of the law, but a judge.

## James 5:9

Grudge not one against another, brethren, lest ye be condemned: behold, the judge standeth before the door.

## James 5:16

Confess your faults one to another, and pray one for another, that ye may be healed. The effectual fervent prayer of a righteous man availeth much.

## I Peter 1:22

Seeing ye have purified your souls in obeying the truth through the Spirit unto unfeigned love of the brethren, see that ye love one another with a pure heart fervently.

## 1 Peter 3:8-9

Finally, be ye all of one mind, having compassion one of another, love as brethren, be pitiful, be courteous: Not rendering evil for evil, or railing for railing: but contrariwise blessing; knowing that ye are thereunto called that ye should inherit a blessing.

## 1 Peter 4:9

Use hospitality one to another without grudging.

## 1 Peter 4:10

As every man hath received the gift, even so minister the same one to another, as good stewards of the manifold grace of God.

## 1 Peter 5:5

Likewise, ye younger, submit yourselves unto the elder. Yea, all of you be subject one to another, and be clothed with humility: for God resisteth the proud, and giveth grace to the humble.

## 1 John 1:7

But if we walk in the light, as he is in the light, we have fellowship one with another, and the blood of Jesus Christ his Son cleanseth us from all sin

# OTHER BOOKS BY JEANETTA BRITT

## Exciting Fiction

Pickin' Ground (The Lottie Series—Book One)
ISBN 978-1-7327071-1-5
In Due Season (The Lottie Series—Book Two)
ISBN 978-1-7327071-2-2
Lottie (The Lottie Series—Book Three)
ISBN 978-1-7327071-3-9
Empty Envelope
ISBN 978-0-9712363-5-6
W.O.O.F (Women of Overcoming Faith)
ISBN 978-1-7327071-4-6
Living in the Seventh Day
ISBN 978-0-6923005-0-3
Dipped in the Fire (The Fire Series—Book One)
ISBN 978-0-6923005-0-3
Double-Dipped in the Fire (The Fire Series—Book Two)
ISBN 978-1-7327071-0-8

## Inspiring Poetry

Glimpses: Poems of Praise (ebook only)
The Collection (poems of praise) (ebook only)
Flittin' & Flyin' (poems on death, birth & life)
ISBN 978-0-9712363-9-4
Under the Influence—Spoken Praise
ISBN 978-0-9712363-7-2
Poems From the Fast
ISBN 978-0-9712363-0-5
Reunion
ISBN 978-0-9712363-1-3
Third Ear
ISBN 978-0-9712363-2-1

## Visit Jeanetta Online

<u>Amazon—Buy Now</u>
http://bit.ly/JBrittBooks

<u>Website</u>
http://www.jbrittbooks.com

https://www.facebook.com/JBrittBooks/
Twitter: @JBrittBooks

# ABOUT THE AUTHOR

Jeanetta Britt is a bestselling author who graduated with honors from Fisk University and The University of Michigan. Her passion for writing contemporary Christian Fiction novels—filled with lots of juicy drama and suspense—as well as, Gospel poetry, surfaced in 1996 and has grown steadily since that time. "While being swept up in the story," Jeanetta says, "I want my readers to *feel* the love of Jesus and find refuge in Him, like I did."

After completing a rewarding professional career in public administration in Dallas, Texas, Jeanetta returned to her native Alabama to write and to live. Her southern roots are reflected in her strong imagery, memorable characters, and delightfully witty storytelling style. She is a sought-after inspirational speaker, by youth and adults alike, with eight novels and seven books of poetry to her credit.

Jeanetta is also an avid gardener, and she founded Twelve Stones CDC—a non-profit organization that operates two community gardens in rural Alabama. "We provide free, fresh food for our community and an opportunity for our youth and senior citizens to form vital intergenerational bonds, and to get some free exercise, companionship and sunshine, too," she says. "No rules— just love!"

.